WAVELAND

WAVELAND

A NOVEL

FREDERICK BARTHELME

Doubleday

New York London Toronto

Sydney Auckland

ⅅⅅ

DOUBLEDAY

Published in the United States by Doubleday, an imprint of
The Doubleday Publishing Group, a division of
Random House, Inc., New York.
www.doubleday.com

Book design by Michael Collica

Library of Congress Cataloging-in-Publication Data
Barthelme, Frederick, 1943–
Waveland: a novel by Frederick Barthelme. —1st ed.
p. cm.
1. Divorced people—Fiction. 2. Roommates—Fiction.
3. Triangles (Interpersonal relations)—Fiction. 4. Gulf Coast
(Miss.)—Fiction. 5. Domestic fiction. I. Title.
PS3552.A763W38 2009
813'.54—dc22
2008013511

ISBN 978-0-385-52729-3

1 3 5 7 9 10 8 6 4 2

First Edition

For Rie

WAVELAND

1

A year after Katrina swept across the Mississippi Gulf Coast and destroyed everything in or near its path, Vaughn Williams was spending a quiet fall afternoon with the television, waiting for his new girlfriend, Greta Del Mar, to get home from work. It was raining and out the window of Greta's bungalow, where he'd been living for the last two months, he could still see the devastation of the landscape—*everything* was gone, vanished, flattened. Three houses on this block of Mary Magdalene Street survived, a few others spotted the landscape here and there, but the rest were leveled. Waveland looked like one of those unpopulated atolls in the Pacific people were always doing TV specials about. Bombing range stuff. By now, a year after the storm, there were a few trailers up on concrete blocks, some tents hooked onto pickups, but that was it. He and Greta were like shipwreck victims washed up on some blown-out shore. Vaughn was ten years older than Greta, both of them split from their spouses—he by divorce, she by the still-unsolved killing of her husband, Bo, a half-decade before. He'd been shot in the head in his sleep. Their marriage hadn't been pretty, stuffed with Bo's infidelities, abuse, ridicule, and embarrassment, but worse was the aftermath, when Greta was indicted for the crime. She was exonerated, of course, and the charges were dismissed; but too much damage was already done.

Vaughn was padding around the house in gray-bottomed athletic socks that slid a little with each step on the hardwood floor, a floor where dust could be seen when hit at just the right angle by sunlight slanting in the double-hung windows of the place, which was not quite arts and crafts (more like Sears & Roebuck), but still attractive, charming, a soft place to land if you had to land somewhere. Vaughn had needed just such a place after his wife, Gail, invited him to gather his things and go. "Why don't you just move along," she had said one day a month after Katrina, giving him the most dismissive flick of the wrist, as if the gesture itself, less pronounced than the shooing of a fly, said all that needed saying about him, about her, and about them, after twenty years of marriage.

Since that time he'd done little work of any kind, holed up in a couple of dinky apartments, stayed to himself a good deal, bought a trombone, then a drum kit—a modern one, all rubber pads and pickups, wired directly into an amplifier and from there into a set of very fine headphones. He tried going to bars, restaurants, clubs—wherever there were other people—but that hadn't worked so well. Finally, in summer, he met Greta at an Escaped Women's Slave Narratives lecture at the Gulfport College for the Demented (not its real name) where he sometimes taught a course in architectural appreciation, architecture having been his lifelong interest, not to mention occupation, not to mention downfall.

He had just moved from the wooden chair at the small table where the laptop computer sat to the sofa across from the old-fashioned "big screen" TV, a rear-projection unit of about fifty inches he reckoned, though he'd never measured, when the phone rang. It was his ex-wife, Gail, calling.

"Your dangerous girlfriend is in the newspaper," she said. "It's the anniversary of her notorious moment and they're revisiting the case. She's prominently featured—a wedding photo, a court photo, the infamous bracelet."

"You always have such good news," Vaughn said.

"I didn't pick her," Gail said. "Is she there? Can you talk?"

"I can always talk. And no, she's not here."

"The photo doesn't look much like her. That's a plus. I mean, she won't be recognized from it. I wouldn't recognize her. But the story is crazy. Jesus."

"I explained the story already," he said.

"Yeah, but you left out the gory details. It's totally ick."

"It is, but it had nothing to do with her. The guy was a creep. He had creepy friends. He got shot one night. They tried to get her for it and couldn't come up with anything."

"I know," Gail said. "The newspaper carefully says, 'Investigators found insufficient evidence to link Mrs. Del Mar to the crime.' Still, I mean, who ever knows about this kind of thing?"

"Gail?" he said. "State your business."

"Okay. Sorry. It's just nervous-making, you know? People you run into and all that. So forget I mentioned it. What I was calling about was your birthday. I was thinking maybe we could have dinner. You know—celebrate."

3

"This is only the third time you've called in a year," Vaughn said.

"I am aware of that, Vaughn."

"Last time was when the grinder pump in the sewage lift station went."

"I know. I'm sorry. But we really should celebrate your birthday," she said.

His birthday was a couple of weeks away, but she wanted to set up the dinner sooner, in the next few days, because she was thinking she might be out of town later. She said, "We ought to carry on at least one tradition from our marriage, which failed so abruptly."

"I remember that," he said.

"C'mon," she said. "It'll be fun."

It wasn't something he wanted to do. He was thinking that once you get through with people, you really don't want to get involved with them again.

"It might be kind of awkward," he said. "You know, Greta and everything."

"I'm fine with that," she said. "I won't say a word about anything. It'll be good to see you again. I think about you a lot these days."

"You do?" he said, thinking how dumb that sounded, how *What? Me Worry?,* wondering why he couldn't at least fake something appropriate.

"I'm taking you guys to the Palomino," she said. "You been there?"

"We saw a TV show about it," he said. "It's the new place in the Beau Rivage, right?"

"It's nice," Gail said. "I mean it's garish and stupid, but as nice as, you know, garish and stupid gets."

The Beau Rivage was the first casino to reopen after the storm. It had escaped pretty much unharmed, and the rebuild was quick and easy. A year after Katrina most of the casinos were still shut up tight.

"How about eight-thirty?" Gail said. "Monday? Oh, and have you heard from Newton?"

Newton was Vaughn's brother, and Vaughn had not heard from him. He never heard from Newton. They didn't get along that well, which she knew. Gail had dated Newton before she and Vaughn started seeing each other. That's how they met, through Newton. Then they got married and she didn't talk about Newton, even when Vaughn asked.

"I haven't heard a peep out of him," Vaughn said. "I guess he's still succeeding a mile a minute up in the Great Northwest."

"Oops," she said. "I forgot. Things are no better, huh?"

"Same as ever," he said.

"I never forget your voice, you know? I mean, calling today you sound just like you. It's great. You know how people sound different when you haven't talked to them in a long time? Not you, Vaughn."

"Good to know," he said.

"So, Monday?"

"We'll be there," he said, and then, when he heard her disconnect, he replaced the receiver and lifted his hands to heaven.

Vaughn flipped over to a cooking channel and stared at the food on the big screen of Greta's big TV. They'd been together since mid-summer and he had started to think of her as his first girlfriend since the marriage. She had this difficult past. The dead husband shot in her bed—a single shot to the head, twenty-two caliber. She inherited a good deal of money. No one was ever tried and the case remained unsolved. She'd shown Vaughn the newspaper clippings from the time of the murder. There were plenty of clippings. It was a big deal in the coast newspapers then, but she was matter-of-fact about it now. How she came home, how she found him, how she felt seeing him dead. What it was like being the prime suspect, the target of endless police interviews, the topic of idiot newspaper stories that got almost everything wrong. Later she sold the house, moved west along the Gulf Coast, set herself up in the bungalow in Bay St. Louis that she'd gotten through her family. The odd part was that she missed the husband, Bo, even though he was a rat of a guy.

Vaughn and Greta were starting slow. He was older, not in such a rush, and she was pretty in a beat-up way, kind of a casualty. Their romance did not scorch the sheets, but they had a good time together. They were calm, they were quiet, they went easy, which freed them from many imperatives.

The rain had gotten louder. It was splattering against the windows, great swaths of water coursing down the glass in pretty ways. The sandwich on TV was the size of a wheelbarrow. It was bright and smeary. He got a fresh Coke from the kitchen, then settled in at the computer and started Googling things—"Del Mar murder" pulled up a few things, then "sex crimes" produced three million hits, including one that offered to "map sex offenders in my local area" and "find registered sexual predators in our free national registry." Then he tried "Macao" because it was in a movie they'd seen recently, and after that he read something about Leonardo DiCaprio, then looked up the Palomino, found the menu online. The baked potato was thirteen-fifty.

He and Gail had split up a couple of months after Katrina, and ever since he'd been trying to be friendly to everybody, across the board, because it made him feel better. He didn't know why, it just hit him that way. He had known the marriage was gone before it went, but actually splitting up gave him this whole new appreciation of things. He wanted to be easygoing and relaxed. He didn't want to feel so apart from people. That had been okay when he and Gail were together, but not after. And when Gail asked him to leave, he realized how important it was going to be to be nice. He had a hard time with her resolve, the sense he had that it really was done between them, there was no going back, no cooling off, no changing of minds, none of the usual ways out of hard moments. She was done and it was clear. There were no options.

She said she needed to find herself, needed to move on with her life, and other things people say when they can't bear to say what's bothering them; but worse than that was the not letting up. Usually people said the bitter stuff first and got it out, got it on the floor there between them, and then stepped away, allowing a little room, and pretty soon everybody had a chance. This wasn't like that. They'd been married a long time and this was steely. She wasn't kidding; she wasn't giving. There was no room. Seeing this unreachable part of her after all those years terrified him.

He moved to a motel in town for a week or two, then to an apartment. Then he went back to the house and she had already divvied everything up—his stuff was in the dining room and the garage. She'd done a good job. He rented a truck and got two good-natured students from the architecture program to load and move the stuff.

The separation made a believer out of him. Almost immediately he tried to put the nice-guy thing into practice. He started having conversations in stores with strangers. Not elaborate conversations, just a few words here and there, shared recognition, that sort of thing. That was new for him. Mostly he had been quiet and removed. When he had worked in architectural firms, he was always looking out for the details of whatever was being done; he was the guy who was interested in the work and not the people doing the work. That went out the window.

He was teaching the semester after the storm, and he spent a lot of time at the school, which was some distance inland. It had been hit, but not hard enough to shut it down for longer than a week or two. He cleaned up his office and hung some new pictures, talked hurricane with the other faculty, delivered food, checked houses, helped with various recovery projects, went to a couple of school functions. He had conferences with his students, who he didn't know that well. He kept telling them to come by for conferences. He kept way more office hours than made any sense. And he spent some time in his office at night, which was odd, because the offices at the school were the worst—old, endlessly repainted, too bright. He found the place consoling somehow. It was stark, but there were trees outside, and it was wonderfully deserted at night, so it was like living in a bad painting, slightly surreal. He didn't know what was going on. Maybe he was trying to change his personality so Gail would get the idea that there were possibilities after all. He didn't plan that, but that's what it looked like in hindsight. It didn't work. But the students seemed to like the new Vaughn better than the old caustic and chilly Vaughn, so the change was half a success.

Even before Katrina, when Waveland was all there, it wasn't a high-toned beachfront town; it was more like ten miles of down-on-its-luck trailer park. After the storm it was ten miles of debris, snapped telephone poles, shredded sheets in the trees. More than a year later there were only a couple of new houses on the beach highway where doctor-types had picked up the distressed property, the better to spend a couple of weekends each summer looking at the Mississippi Sound, a muddy sump you could walk straight out into for a mile and the water wouldn't rise much above your ankles. The town was mostly empty lots, loose rubble, FEMA trailers sprouting yellow extension cords, tents, garbage, and lots of photo opportunities—boats standing on their noses, cars jackknifed, garages flattened like cardboard boxes. The media people had stayed maybe a week or two after the storm before fleeing for the sexier story in New Orleans—death on the rooftops, Sean Penn in the water up to his pecs. On the Mississippi coast recovery was ridiculously slow, almost nonexistent. There wasn't much to recover since there wasn't much *there* anymore, just flattened houses and empty lots piled with rubbish and wreckage. The Waveland city elders were talking about becoming part of Bay St. Louis, the next town east.

The beach road curved out to a dead end ten miles west. There were a half-dozen stilt houses still on the road; the rest had been blown to smithereens. A mile inland another highway slanted up to Interstate 10 in the west and, going east, ran across the bay to Pass Christian, Gulfport, and Biloxi. Only now the bridge was all pilings and no roadway. Waveland was like Baghdad if the Air Force had hit it really hard—gone. Where property had been spared by the storm, most businesses were boarded up. The nearest gas station had one functioning island, clogged toilets, and soap dispensers half full of pink goo and dripping. There were no locks on any doors, where there were doors.

The divorce was as pristine as could be. A delicate trading of papers conducted through lawyers they picked out of the Yellow Pages. When they saw each other, Vaughn wept, and Gail did not weep. She was the poster girl for lack of affect. She wasn't nasty, though; she was sensible as they went about the division of things, but this made him feel worse. He was shocked at everything—at being alone, shunted back to living as if he were twenty-five, at how much time there was in a day, at the way the air went still if he wasn't disturbing it. Occasionally he went into frenzy mode, cleaning everything in sight in his apartment, straightening furniture, polishing silverware, vacuuming the floors again and again, and that was satisfying, but it didn't last. He liked things clean, so there was always plenty to do, but his enthusiasm waned.

They set out to make the divorce simple, but the way it actually went off, by mail and telephone, with lawyers they barely knew, it was like a drive-through deal, almost as though they'd never been married in the first place. Before he knew it, the legal stuff was over and he was in his second new apartment and she was at the house and three months had gone by. Papers came in the mail. He signed them and pushed them back into the return envelope. The envelope was gray. The world was different. Days were longer, nights were unbearable. Sleep was a paradise.

When he told Greta about the birthday dinner, she said, "Fine." She had just come in the kitchen door and he'd met her there, so they were standing in the kitchen. He went to the sink and washed his hands using the dishwashing liquid, which had a filmy feel to it.

"Maybe she wants something else, maybe she has some ideas," he said.

"Don't you get started," Greta said.

"She wouldn't call if she didn't want something."

"Maybe she's lonely. Maybe she wanted to wish you Happy Birthday."

"Well, sure," he said. "But I talked to her like once in the last year and now she wants to take us out to dinner."

"I talked to her more than you did," Greta said. This was true. After Vaughn introduced Greta, back in the summer, she and Gail became phone pals for a while. "We're buds."

"You're in the paper, apparently," he said. "Gail said she read it. Pictures, the whole thing."

"I know," Greta said. "It'll pass. I have it in the car if you want to read it. I was going to bring it in, but I guess I thought maybe we could just skip it."

"Fine by me," Vaughn said. "There's no point in shooting *me* anyway."

"Funny," she said.

"So, anyway, we've got to go to dinner with Gail, and

I'm thinking she's got an ulterior motive, something up her sleeve."

He could almost hear Greta rolling her eyes. "I hate to tell you this," Greta said, "but I think she's over the divorce and ready to be friends again. It'll be fine."

"What about me?"

"You are not over the divorce, but you'll be fine, too, eventually. You can do this, Vaughn. You're the man. You're Mr. Nice Guy."

"Thanks," he said. This was Greta's final answer to his idea of a new personality. She used it all the time.

"You should stop worrying. It'll be easy and pleasant, and anyway, it would be better if you and she talked more—you know, like friends or something."

"Okay. We'll have a nice dinner and all that. It won't be so bad. You'll go with me, right? And we're not worrying about it."

"Now you're talking," Greta said. "I wouldn't miss it. But right now I'm going to yoga."

"You are? You just got home."

"It's okay, Vaughn. I'm coming back afterward." She kissed his cheek, picked up her yoga gear, and left again.

He watched her back out of the driveway and then went to the computer and tried a more general search: "husband killers." One million seven hundred and eighty thousand entries in six-tenths of a second. He read a few of those, including "I fight my husband's killer with laughter" and several other choice headlines. Then he tried "beheadings," which produced eight hundred and twenty-one thousand hits and numerous videos. He started a couple of those, then gave it up. Years before he'd been interested in grotesque news, had put together a site that featured news like the woman who cooked her husband in a pot, the couple who kept their dead relatives in plastic bags, the father who buried his child to the neck in ants. There was a surprising amount of that going on, he discovered, then, as now; only now he wasn't that intrigued. Now he was thinking: With Google, why bother with school?

He did a vanity search and found references to buildings he'd worked on for architects here and there, and one entry for a monograph he'd cowritten in college on the work of Bruce Goff and Herb Greene. It was available at a used bookstore in Arkansas.

Eventually he gave up on the computer and went back to the television, letting the broadcasts wash over him. There was too much of everything. He flipped between a show on illegal aliens and another show on the child sex trade in Cambodia, both reruns. The Cambodia show featured a touchy dentist from the States who was tricked in Phnom Penh into talking about how he liked to take seven-year-olds to his hotel room.

"These children are so dear to me," this guy said in his tissuey little voice. "I have visited this nation several times a year since I first started coming in the nineteen-eighties, and it is such a lovely country, such sweet people."

Vaughn felt sorry for the guy, this earnest pedophile. He was being kneecapped by the TV people and didn't seem to understand that; he just kept on confessing. But he deserved to be kneecapped, so Vaughn settled in to watch, thinking of the guy's family and loved ones, the people who depended on him and who cared for him back in Lincoln, Nebraska, or Continent, Georgia. He was a creepy little man, all hair and no forehead. He seemed to have a constant and insatiable hankering for the Cambodian boys, but on this day he was the star of the show. He was pleased. He was smiling. He was the pedophile unfairly tricked by cruel documentary filmmakers, a case study in the modern.

2

Greta had the rode-hard-and-put-up-wet look that he was a sucker for—a look few women could pull off because, if you had it, you were traveling so close to skanky, cheap, and beat down all the time that it was easy to mistake one for the other. But she had it mastered; she never missed. Before the husband, her family was a story. Father died when she was a kid. Raised by her mother, single parent, messy childhood and adolescence, small college to study interior design; then her mother died and left her a little pile of cash and the bungalow in Waveland. She didn't like her mother much but was grateful for the leavings. Then the marriage, then that went haywire and she moved to Waveland, where she restored the house to its original specs, cleaning things up; but then Katrina arrived. The house got a few trees through the roof and lost a wall, but she was invested in it so was quick to do the repairs.

Vaughn had run into her when hunting apartments at the beginning of the summer. She was renting her renovated garage; he was the first tenant. They had architecture in common—she was doing small jobs for people with old houses along the coast. He'd trained in architecture at Tulane and Yale, in the Goeters years when the idea was, How do we burn down the architecture school this week? Afterward he'd worked in big and none-too-good offices in Atlanta and Dallas, and elsewhere, and had finally more or less retired to the coast of Mississippi to get away from the business. Gail was with him for most of the trek. They had some money saved, and he was going to pick up some work along the coast. Beach houses, he was thinking. That was the idea. It never quite worked out the way he planned.

The courtship with Greta was offhand. They started going to dinner, going to stores together, seeing movies, trading ideas for her ongoing renovation of the house. That put them together a lot of the time. He was glad, too, because most of the time since he and Gail split had been dreary, as though the light was always filtered through tarps.

One night he and Greta had dinner at Sun Deluxe, a tiny Chinese place run by two Vietnamese women, a typical coastal place—a whitewashed repurposed Exxon station with mismatched booths and flat silver ashtrays, the tables covered in strangely textured red plastic, sticky paper napkins, cheap chopsticks, jars of orange sauce on the table, an all-you-can-eat buffet every night, and no customers. They had an especially good time, and when they got back to her house, Greta invited him in and showed him a bedroom she said he could have if he wanted it.

"You could stay here," she said.

"Here?"

"Inside," she said. "Not a big thing, just instead of having to go out there all the time, I mean. Unless . . ."

"No, no," he said. "I got it. I'm there. Let me get my stuff."

So he moved into the house, and Greta rented the apartment to a one-handed white guy named Eddie who was a veteran of the first Gulf War and an acquaintance of hers. He told Vaughn he was gay. He was a nasty-looking thing with cartoon hair, stuck up straight as licorice sticks, and a fondness for Hawaiian shirts, of which he seemed to have a good supply. He seemed like trouble, like he could take care of himself and he'd do it at your expense. He stared, unblinking, always looking straight at you, pressure in those eyes. The night he came to see the apartment, Greta came back inside after showing the apartment and said, "He's one of those off-the-books military types they send in for the sterile fatigue stuff."

"Why rent him the place?"

"Like him," she said. "He's on our side, you know?"

"Grand," Vaughn said.

"He's taking you out for beer," she said.

"When?"

"Now," she said. "I told him you'd go with."

They went to a local bar called Hot-2-Trot. It was a place Vaughn and Greta had gone a few times, off the beach near Central Avenue, the leveled main street in Waveland. Eddie wanted a nightcap. "Just one drink," he said.

He got drunk. When he was drunk he asked Vaughn to kiss him, and Vaughn said, "No. And you'd best be careful, as I am friends with the landlady."

"Heard that," Eddie said. "Miss Greta. She's good."

"You know her?"

"Oh . . . no, not really. I mean, sorta. I worked some job of hers a couple times, landscape stuff, construction. Hey— c'mon. Give us a little peck on the cheek."

"I don't kiss people anymore," Vaughn said, trying to steer clear of any kind of trouble. He figured Eddie was testing him.

Eddie had giant pruney lips. He was a percussionist before he lost the hand.

"Wingy Manone," Vaughn said, remembering the one- armed trumpet genius from some book his brother, Newton, read when they were kids.

"Shit," Eddie said, and he frowned, as if Vaughn's saying it was crude and insensitive.

Vaughn started to apologize, and suddenly Eddie leaned over and kissed him. Sloppy, on the lips, his moustache scrap- ing Vaughn's upper lip, Eddie's lips grabbing his like some snap-on tool. There wasn't anything Vaughn could do.

Vaughn figured Eddie was screwing with him, or maybe Eddie *was* gay and wanted to prove it to everybody every minute.

"Gotcha," Eddie said, smirking, turning back to his Lone Star.

"That's it," Vaughn said. He wiped his mouth elaborately. "Maybe try brushing next time."

"Now, if you'd just pecked me, like right here"—Eddie tapped his lips, which looked like a pair of liver-colored shrimp bunk-bedding on the bottom of his face—"if you pecked me like I asked, you'd have been home free."

Eddie had a fancy one-handed cigarette-lighting trick. He

did it and then looked to Vaughn for approval. "I can do it with no hands, too," he said. "Like that guy in *Freaks*."

"People been doing that since that movie came out," Vaughn said. "The forties or something. That guy had *no* arms."

"Guy was a laundry bundle," Eddie said. "But I'm bringing the trick back." He made a big smoke cloud. "They're killing cigarettes here," he said. "Next month or something. I'll have to go outside."

"You can deal with it."

"So what's with you and Greta?" Eddie said. "You moved on up? That the thing?"

"We're friends," Vaughn said. "We're seeing each other."

"Oh, now that's nicely put."

"I don't think I like you all that much," Vaughn said.

"You haven't had my best stuff yet," Eddie said.

They got more beer, and Eddie started telling Vaughn about the war. "It's like the minute I saw those people over there playing drop-the-goat I knew we were in trouble. I mean, *drop-the-goat.* Right there, you know? You do not want to fuck with people who play ball games using an animal as the ball."

"Yeah," Vaughn said.

"It's a question of reverence for life," Eddie said. "Of course when I was over there we toasted those people trying to get back into Iraq from Kuwait. That wasn't our best moment."

"I saw that," Vaughn said.

"But you know we're overmatched, right? Those people are, all of them, crazy. They're all 'I want to bathe in blood' and shit like that."

A tall man in the back said, "Hey! Quiet down, will you?"

Eddie turned around and looked at the guy and pointed his stump back there into the darkness. "Yes sir," he said. "Quiet as a mouse, sir."

"You about ready to go?" Vaughn asked.

"We got no business being there," Eddie said. "It's fucking insane. People'll cut you up and eat you, you don't watch out."

"Not us," Vaughn said. "You did yours. I'm too old."

That got Eddie headed in a new direction. "I hear your whole damn world disintegrated. Wife left you, you got fired, laid off, you got no job, you cruise around eating Chinese food with your landlord, observing the takeover of your world by younger, less capable guys. By children," he said.

"That the deal?"

"Fucking Mike Wallace here," Vaughn said, getting off the stool. "Let's go, huh?"

Eddie pointed to the girl bartender who was leaning over dead ahead, facing the other way. "See this tattoo?" he said, meaning the scrollwork just above her ass. "This is the defining mark of our historical moment. God Bless 'em. Everywhere you go. And they all got this idea at the same time. It's amazing."

"Tramp-stamp," Vaughn said.

"What?"

"What it's called," Vaughn said. "Was in the AARP newsletter."

He pulled Eddie away from the bar, said they had to get back, that Greta was waiting on them. Eddie went willingly, and Vaughn dropped him in the driveway and watched him tilt toward the apartment at the end of the drive.

3

The afternoon of the birthday dinner Vaughn headed for the bathroom to clean up, and Greta's dog, Monkey, seesawed off the couch and clicked into the bathroom after him, then sprawled on the floor by the back corner of the tub. Vaughn figured Monkey liked the sound of running water. Vaughn ran water then got in the tub, his feet up on the edge of the porcelain on either side of the faucet. He had a *Consumer Reports* with "Unbiased Ratings: 333 Products" emblazoned on its cover. There were pictures of cars, televisions, telephones, tires, digital cameras, and something that looked as if it might be an insurance policy. He drew the cover close to his face trying to read the type on the photograph of the contract or policy or whatever it was, but could not. He opened the magazine to the table of contents, and there was the same image again, repeated larger this time. It was a will. The issue had a comparison of will-making software. He started looking at that, but then caught an article on page twelve called "Dangerous Products, a *CR* Investigation." He went there instead, where he found a picture of a flame shooting out of some guy's hand. The caption said, "When we sprayed this aerosol hair glitter on a fire, it shot flames. We bought it in a store's children's party section."

"Perhaps if you hadn't sprayed the fire?" Vaughn said. Monkey did not stir.

Vaughn had trouble reading. He often read in the tub, magazines mostly, but he skipped most of the text, reading a little at the beginning of a paragraph, then moving on to the next paragraph. Often he'd go through an entire article this way, looking at several pages but reading only a sentence or two per paragraph. He wondered if it was ADD.

"Earlier this year *Consumer Reports* revealed that millions of unsafe, recalled products remain in consumer hands," he read. "Dollar shops and closeout stores have been prime destinations for shoddy products," he read. "Electrical products," he read. "Hazardous toys have been a concern since the Toy Industry Association first brought the matter to the attention of the Senate in 1997," he read.

Pretty soon he tossed the magazine and his reading glasses on the bath mat and slid down in the tub until he was covered up to his chin in warm water. He closed his eyes and let the steady drip of the faucet lull him to sleep.

The restaurant that night was all about fat leather seats, dark wood, bright polished copper, waiters and waitresses in starched white shirts, steaks at eighty dollars a pop. Most of the customers had their meals comped. It was dark and chilly in the restaurant, but the bread, which came seconds after they were seated, was toasty.

The greetings were overdone. Hugs and kisses all around. Gail and Greta might have been sorority sisters. Gail had a new look, thin and taller than he remembered, wearing a leather jacket, a long scarf, Beatle boots. She wore black jeans and looked quite severe with a new haircut, also black. Her nose was a little more prominent than she might want. Still, she was handsome and looked younger than she was. She could have passed for forty. Greta was dressed like a cowgirl—jeans and an open-collar man's button-down shirt, and she was less thin than Gail.

"So, it's just the three of us then?" Greta said.

"I guess," Gail said. She reached into her purse and pulled out a folded section of newspaper. "Your press," she said to Greta, sliding the paper to her.

"Gee, thanks," Greta said. "We spent some time on that already. If you have a cat you might want to keep it?"

Gail grinned. "Well, you know—no such thing as bad publicity?"

"There's the murder exception," Vaughn said.

Gail reached for the paper. "I withdraw the offering," she said.

"It's fine," Greta said, capturing the newspaper. "I guess I can keep two copies. It's sort of glamorous, don't you agree?"

"Terribly," Gail said.

"It's not every day one dines with the notorious," Vaughn said.

They were seated in a booth, Vaughn on one side of the table and the two women on the other. He saw his past and future in a single glance.

The chat about Greta went on, and Gail and Greta looked friendly—they seemed to "get" each other in some special way. Vaughn just watched and smiled, spun his knife on the tabletop until Gail reached over to stop the knife from twirling. "Vaughn," she said.

"Sorry," he said.

"He does that," Greta said.

"I like to watch talk shows on television, especially political shows," he said. This was his idea for changing the subject.

"Me, too," Gail said. "They're so earnest and dopey—it's hard to imagine who they think they're talking to out here."

"They're *explaining* everything to us," Greta said.

"Talking to themselves," Gail said.

"They've simplified the world for us morons," Greta said.

"What do you think, Vaughn?" Gail said, tapping his hand.

"A world in which I feel more comfortable," he said. "Beautiful and stark."

"Hmm," she said.

"I want to organize alphabetically all the things I hate," he said.

"You're always so organized," Gail said.

"He doesn't hate everything," Greta said to Gail.

"I know," Gail said.

"He just gets upset and angry."

"I know," Gail said.

"There are upsetting things out there, upsetting things happening all the time," Greta said. "I get upset sometimes myself, but then I just let it go."

"Me, too," Gail said.

"He doesn't let it go," Greta said. "He's trying, though."

"Says he is," Gail said, readying her salad for eating. The salads were spare and lovely on shallow white plates, little arrays of lettuces and walnuts. "So what happened to the new you?" Gail said.

"I'm still here," he said. "I just forget sometimes."

They began to eat. They talked all during dinner, nonstop—last year's hurricane, the trash still scattered around, the way it still looked in some places as if the storm had just come through in the last week, the politics of gambling on the coast, the casinos, the usual.

"When they have a war, have they always just reported the number of Americans killed?" Gail said. "I hate that."

"They used to report the number of Americans and the much bigger number of enemies," Vaughn said. "To prove we were winning."

"Stupid war," Greta said. "They should have put Saddam back in charge when they found him."

They talked about Eddie, and Vaughn said Eddie had said he'd worked for Greta, and Greta said yeah, and he had good bona fides, so she didn't mind renting to him. They chatted about what Vaughn was doing for work, which was nothing but a couple of classes at the college, and Gail asked about Newton and Vaughn reminded her that he really didn't know, and then she, naturally, apologized for asking, and said she never really understood why there was so much bad blood between brothers, and Vaughn said there wasn't so much bad

25

blood, it's just that they were different people, and then every-body made faces as if that sounded so lame, so he just waved it off, changed the subject again to ask her about their house, still jointly held, which she said was holding up, and that it had finally gotten the new roof it didn't really need cour-tesy of the insurance company, and then she told Vaughn and Greta about some of her projects, and asked if they'd seen her on TV on the news a month or so before, and they said they hadn't, but wished they had. It was strange how much talk there was, it just seemed to pour out of them and stay neatly away from worrisome spots, too, once they got started, as if all of them knew the territory well. Later, when dinner was over and coffee had been declined, Vaughn reached for the check and Gail rolled her eyes toward the ceiling, stopping him dead. "You got it," he said.

She searched her purse for a card, and as soon as she placed it on the piano-black table, the waiter swooped in like a peregrine. The service was high-speed.

Then they left the restaurant. Gail said, "I'm going to hang out, play awhile."

"Since when?" Vaughn said.

"I do it all the time," she said. "I win a fair bit."

"No kidding? Playing what?"

"Slots," she said. "I play the dollars. If I've got money, I play the fives and tens."

Her hair was raggedy and she was still inviting. The thin-ness made her complicated. He gave her a hug and a kiss high on her cheek and said good night, noticing for the first time that she had the name *Tony* in ink on her neck. He couldn't tell if it was a tattoo or something else.

"What is this?" he said, pointing at her neck.

"A joke," she said. "It says 'Tony.' "

"Yeah, I see it says Tony, but, like, what's it doing there?"

"It's just ballpoint," she said. "I met this guy named Tony. I liked him, so, you know, he wrote on my neck."

"He tattooed his name on your neck?" Vaughn said. "And you left it on there?"

"Well, he just did it this morning," she said. "Last night, really. I'm going to run into him here later. It's just ballpoint."

He turned to Greta. "He did it on there this morning."

"I got that," Greta said.

"It's not a big thing," Gail said. "It's nothing. I'm going to play some slots. I'm going to meet up with him in a bit. Why don't you guys go on? It was great seeing you again, Vaughn. We should do it more often now. I'm really a lot better than I was last year. It's good to see you guys. And Happy Birthday. Really."

"How are you getting home?" he said.

"She's got a car, Vaughn," Greta said.

He felt stupid. "Right," he said. "I lost track there for a minute."

Gail stepped up and hugged Greta, whispered something that he couldn't hear. The two of them smiled, laughed a little, patted each other, then Greta steered Vaughn away, side by side on the ornate casino carpet toward the entrance, the jangling slots and dropping coins and hits-of-all-kinds relentless. At the door he turned and looked back, but Gail had vanished into the crowd, into glitter and smoke. Outside, he and Greta stood under the overhang for a minute. It was chilly, rainy, the first front of the season coming through. They paused a second, then stepped out into the parking lot.

4

Greta had won the fifty-two-inch rear-projection Sony television in a church raffle, a gift to the church from one of the casinos. The casinos, just as you might imagine, were like that, always donating to this or that charity, always being good citizens, always going the extra mile for the local firemen, or police, or PTA. It didn't matter much what your organization was, if you needed a little helping hand, the casinos were always ready. They went out of their way to contribute to the well-being of the community. The casinos were real team players when it came to participating in community affairs, models of selfless commitment to a better life for all.

When Vaughn first saw this TV, back in the summer, he'd said, "I always wanted one of these, but it cost too much and the quality of the screen isn't that good and the image is fuzzy and it's an ugly piece of furniture that takes up too much room.

It's kind of an eyesore. I guess that's why most people avoid 'em." This was the first night he stayed at Greta's place.

"Why, thanks very much," Greta said, making a curious face.

"That's not exactly what I meant," he said.

"I was a fool to accept it," she said.

"C'mon, that's not right," he said. "I just meant that—"

"Yeah, yeah," she'd said. "Okay. I accept your apology."

It was their first big night and Vaughn wasn't 100 percent under control. He tried to repair this gaffe by explaining about rear-projection television, and about DLP rear projection compared to CRT rear projection, and about direct-view CRTs, and the business about scanning, about 1080i and 1080p, and how the picture is composed of alternating lines that are difficult to get in register. After a while he could see that wasn't working.

"I really always wanted one," he said finally.

"He scores!" she said, offering up a high-five.

So they turned the set off and went about their business. He read a book. She regarded him with great curiosity, and then, after a suitable period of observation, said, "What is that strange object you're playing with?"

"Got it," he said. And they went to bed.

The days that followed went more smoothly. Vaughn accepted the television and the television accepted Vaughn.

The night they went to dinner with Gail, however, they returned from the casino restaurant and things weren't going so well. They weren't talking to each other. Eddie was in the house, in the living room, sprawled on the couch, making himself at home, snacking, and watching something that looked like ultimate cage fighting on the big screen.

"Vaughn is upset about his wife," Greta said.

"Yeah?" Eddie said. He didn't take his eyes off the TV.

"She had some guy's name tattooed on her neck," she said.

"Wasn't a tattoo," Vaughn said. "Was an ink thing, like a drawing."

"Even worse," she said. "What kind of guy draws his name on some woman's neck?"

"Young guy," Eddie said, wincing as one fighter on television kneed the other guy repeatedly in the groin. "This is old-time ultimate fighting. They don't let 'em do that anymore."

It surprised Vaughn how pissed he was about Gail. Pissed and sickened—she was a grown woman, well past the age where you get written on. He tried to hide the anger, but Greta was all over it and she wasn't pleased. They'd ridden in silence from the casino, watching the wipers slog back and forth across the windshield.

"What're you doing in here anyway?" he said to Eddie. "Don't you have a TV out in the apartment?"

"Tiny screen," Eddie said. "Barely see it. These guys would be the size of squirrels on it. The size of nuts. Couldn't see the action. It's part of my rental agreement."

Vaughn turned to Greta.

"What?" she said. "I told him he could use the TV when we weren't using it."

"Weird," Vaughn said.

"You said if you weren't here I could use the television," Eddie said. He was gathering his stuff around him, not picking it up, but moving it closer to himself.

"He's right. That's true. I said that," Greta said.

"Well, we're here now," Vaughn said. "There's a ring on the floor there where your beer is." He sniffed the air. "It smells like smoke in here. You been smoking?"

"I haven't smoked a single thing," Eddie said. "Loosen up, will you?"

"It's the boyfriend," Greta said, stage-whispering. She was standing in the doorway between the den and the hall that led to her bedroom, unbuttoning her blouse.

"What are you doing?" Vaughn said. "With the shirt? Would you mind?"

She sighed. "What? It's going to upset him? He's . . . you know?"

"Yeah," Eddie said. "I'm—"

"Oh, please," Vaughn said.

"Well, pardon me, Mr. Rockefeller," she said. She waved at Eddie, then went down the hall, her footsteps ringing.

Vaughn sat in the chair alongside the couch and stared at the screen. The captioning was on, and the picture-in-picture was on. The sound was off. By now Eddie had changed channels a couple of times. There was an ad for some kind of mini-tractor on the screen—a guy picking up leaves, hauling them around his yard, vacuuming them into some kind of cloth bin that was pulled behind the tractor. This image was duplicated in the inset window on the screen.

"Why are you watching the same thing twice?" Vaughn said.

"I like it," Eddie said.

"You like what?" Vaughn said.

"The two pictures," Eddie said. "I like two pictures together."

31

"It's the same picture," Vaughn said. "The two pictures are the same."

"I know that," Eddie said. "I can see them better when there're two of them."

"You like that they're the same. I get it. It's fine. It's very attractive," Vaughn said.

"It's what I like," Eddie said.

A fire blazed in duplicate on the giant screen. "What're we watching here?" Vaughn said.

"Fire," Eddie said.

"I see that, but what?" Vaughn said.

"Ad. Fireplaces, maybe. Colorful fire logs. Insurance. I don't know what. I was watching a rerun of *CSI* before. That's the most popular show on television. That guy on there is really bowlegged."

"He's the most bowlegged guy on television," Vaughn said.

"I guess," Eddie said. "I like that blond woman—she's kind of sexy. And then there's that other woman on there—that black-haired woman? She's kind of sexy. And I like the special effects. I like it when they get that blue light out and start looking at things," Eddie said. "They always find sperm, you know? Every week they pull out the blue light and find some sperm. It's a hoot."

"That's so last year," Vaughn said. "Finding sperm."

Eddie started flipping through the channels. He stopped on a "Healthier You" ad, some movie with a bunch of British people in it, an HBO channel with a cowboy movie. He flipped backward to get to The Weather Channel and then went through *Robot Wars,* public affairs, the shopping network, and a *Matlock* rerun.

"It doesn't look too good now," Eddie said.

"Keep moving," Vaughn said. "You'll find something."

Eddie kept clicking, the channel changing simultaneously in both windows. He passed *Animal Planet* with the world's biggest and baddest bugs, some other stuff, and then he paused and said, "You worried about your wife?"

Vaughn stared at him for a minute or more. "Well," he finally said. "Sure. I haven't seen her in a year and . . . I don't know. You always worry about the ex-wife, don't you? It's built in, goes with the territory."

"I ain't worried about mine," Eddie said.

"I didn't know you had a wife," Vaughn said.

"What, you think I can't handle a wife? I'm not just a faggot, you know. I had a wife once. Just like you. Same thing."

There were puppets on the TV, kids playing with hand puppets. Vaughn thought it was peculiar and wanted to say something but then thought better of it. "My wife had this guy's name on her neck. It hit me the wrong way," he said.

"That happens," Eddie said. He sat up on the couch and pulled up his socks and began putting on his shoes. Vaughn figured he was getting ready to leave and go back to the garage apartment. He didn't want Eddie to go.

"I didn't ask how it got there," he said. "But I can imagine."

"How old a woman is your wife?" Eddie said.

"Not too old," Vaughn said. "And she looks younger. She's forty-something." He knew exactly how old she was, when her birthday was, but for some reason he said this other thing. So then he said, "Forty-four. In the spring. Looks forty, maybe. She's well preserved. She exercises."

Eddie moved the little square with the second picture in it to different positions on the screen—to the bottom right, to the top right, to the top left, to the bottom left, then back to the bottom right. Then he clicked up the cable schedule and started jumping through that four or five lines at a time. *The Son of Frankenstein* went by, *Intimate Portraits* went by, *Beverly Hills Cop* went by, *Classic Boxing.*

"She doesn't look that old. She looks young, really. She looks good. I figure the guy who wrote on her neck is younger, a kid."

"Maybe he's a lighthearted older guy," Eddie said. "Maybe he's an easy guy to get along with. Maybe he was just having some fun. Maybe they were just joking around. Maybe it wasn't anything."

"That's the ticket," Vaughn said.

"Maybe it was a woman?" Eddie said. "Maybe your wife is joining a club or something and her sponsor had to write her name on your wife's neck." Eddie turned around and gave him a look, a raised eyebrow thing that was a parody of hopeful.

"You look like Bubs," Vaughn said. "The guy who was on *The Wire.*"

"I've got some of the attributes," Eddie said. "I'm short a hand. Got a skin problem."

"Your hair isn't as cool as Bubs's hair," Vaughn said.

"Nothing is," Eddie said.

"You'd think you'd get over shit like this, wouldn't you?" Vaughn said. "We're divorced, we're finished, it's over. We go out with my girlfriend, for God's sake."

"That's nothing you ought to be doing. That's going to make you feel bad every time," Eddie said. "Seeing her, I mean. That's what happened to me. I used to go out with my ex. We didn't go anyplace big—gas stations, hamburger joints, barbecue joints. She always made me feel bad. I felt sad as shit. Like stuff had changed. Both of us knew it, but there was nothing we could do. We'd sit there in the car and drink beer and listen to the radio and smoke cigarettes, watch kids zoom in and out of the convenience store." He shook his head. "That was no fun. Reminded me I used to be the kid driving in, jumping out for a six-pack, speeding off somewhere. Now it was me and the ex in the car with nowhere to go. We were killing time. Sitting and drinking, listening to the radio, smoking cigarettes. Waiting for nothing. Waiting to give up. That was crap."

"This was before or after the divorce?" Vaughn said.

"Both," Eddie said. He grabbed his beer, tipped it up, emptied it. Then he looked at it, tossed it up by the neck, and caught it. "By the end I was just one more thing for her to worry about." He groaned and stood up from the couch, pulling his shirt closed.

"I'll tell you what," Eddie said. "After a while it just isn't worth the trouble." He wagged the beer bottle at Vaughn. "If I were doing fortune cookies, that's what I'd put in them. Every one. *After a while it just isn't worth the trouble.* That and *You will have razor-sharp mystical vision today.*"

"That'd be useful," Vaughn said.

"You read the paper?" Eddie said. "The Bracelet Case? They did another piece today. She taking it all right?"

"Seems to be," Vaughn said.

"It's a shame," Eddie said. "Too much for too long."

Vaughn said, "You've known her awhile, huh? You go way back."

"Well, 'known' might be overstating it. But I've been around doing crap work for a while—construction, dirt work—so I

ran into her. Not like I was the contractor on the job or anything." He shook his head and started for the kitchen. "I just
ran into her. She always seemed nice. The crew guys talked a
lot of shit. You know how that is."

"Just thinking," Vaughn said.

"Sure. She's a nice woman. She's all right," Eddie said.
"Gotta go."

Vaughn heard the bottle click as Eddie set it down on the
kitchen countertop next to the sink. He listened as the door
opened and closed, then listened to Monkey's nails ticking
across the kitchen floor as the dog came into the living room
and curled up on the end of the couch.

Vaughn watched the dog's eyes flick up at him, then away.
Monkey did that a couple of times. Vaughn stared at the
screen and listened to the sudden quiet in the house. He could
hear Greta in the bathroom making those little thumps that
can't quite be identified—water on and off, pipes complaining, cabinet doors shutting, bottles settling on a marble vanity,
bad hinges.

He watched an infomercial for some kind of barbecue de-
vice and read the captioning—"It's light; you can even pick
it up." Flames flamed up. "Here's a little gift for you: the
Q-Grill cookbook with our best grilling recipes." He picked
up the remote, started punching the channel button. He got
Cleopatra, some speech on some steps. Richard Burton arrived looking sort of like Bill Clinton. Vaughn kept clicking.
He found a cowboy, a guy selling hair remover, a woman
with a big mouth, a woman with a big nose, a woman with
big stockings on her arms. Then police in Miami dealing with
sick dogs—the stuff just kept going past, one alarming thing
after another—that episode of *Matlock* with a character who

looked like Norman Mailer, the *Girls Still Gone Wild* thing, an infomercial for Jaystone gel bras. The world looked turbulent.

Vaughn couldn't really remember that much about Gail and himself, back when things were good. How they worked, how they stayed together. Or where it had gone. Fifteen years. It might as well have been his parents' life. He had a head full of photographs but not much else. They weren't sharp photographs, either. Vague, ripe for forgetting. Stuff didn't count because it was long over. People said they had sweet memories, but he had only bits and pieces. It was all he could do to remember somebody's name, a place he'd lived. He could remember a door, maybe a balcony, the stove someplace. Not much.

On the screen he caught a stunned-looking alligator with a bowie knife stuck in the back of its head, then the Gateway Arch in St. Louis lit up in pink for breast cancer awareness. It looked good, he thought.

He imagined Tony and Gail at the casino—drinking, smoking, playing the slots, having a good time. Tony was probably some kid cop or something. Some guy she ran into somewhere. One of those greasy restaurant managers he'd always heard about.

He sat in the living room at Greta's house, clicking through the television channels, catching bits of the narrative on the screen. He clicked the muting off, heard "Dizziness and diarrhea" and "Have you met life today?" He tried to remember girls from high school: Sarah Quinn, Phillipa Henry, Terry Hook. He tried to picture them, remember some incident or some moment when they were more than names, when they were objects of intense desire. He got nothing. For a couple of them he got places—stray nights in some car of his father's, or by the lake, or in the girl's parents' garage, or in some den full of puffy furniture, on a stairway, at a piano, the front step—or summer nights, chilly winters, almost surviving memories of kisses, caresses, clothes, scents by pools and in backyards with parties in progress. Girls—with accents, odd dresses, awkward bodies, peculiar ways of using their arms. In Vaughn's memory Gail was already in their company—not as far removed, but the same category. Remember when . . . and who could remember, really? Who could remember more than facts. I slept with this woman. We kissed here. She wore orange. So much stuff shoehorned into this category of memory that there was little to do but be thankful that something was there, occupying that spot named *the past.*

And now he had days filled with things that were annoying in their familiarity, and yet he could not quite remember them—gestures, remarks, fears, anxieties, hopes, plans. So he smiled and told jokes, tried to be friendly, tried to get by. He assumed this was what others were doing, too. Those who had been around awhile. He started thinking that his parents must have done this for years. His mother and father had endured a long, private decline in an apartment, the two of them jammed in there like gerbils, walking upstairs and down, watching television, eating meals together silently, watching more television, going upstairs and downstairs for thirty years or more after retirement. His father had complained. His mother had not complained. And then they died, one after the other.

5

A week later Vaughn, Greta, and Eddie were eating at Sun Deluxe, the Exxon station turned Chinese restaurant. Vaughn had talked to Greta about Eddie and now they were all pals, they were new best friends. They'd been hanging out nonstop. They were complaining about things in their lives, the ways things were going, Greta being tossed around in the paper again, Vaughn's trouble with Gail, Eddie fitting nowhere at all.

"After a while you start thinking stuff isn't too interesting," Vaughn said. "Whatever it is other people are interested in. It's on television and you've seen it all before. Or they tell the story and miss about half of what's important."

"What're you having?" Eddie said. He was flapping the menu with his hand, trying to get it to stay straight.

"When people don't get stuff, it's annoying," Greta said. "It's like they aren't paying attention, usually."

"What're you, an English professor?" Vaughn said.

"It's like you get to a point and it all falls away from you," she said.

"You're not there yet," Vaughn said.

"I am, sorta," she said. "It's all twenty-year-olds now. They get the jobs, they're on TV. What can they do? They don't know anything."

"That's the way people looked at us back when," Vaughn said.

"I want some meat," Eddie said. "Would you guys shut up and order?"

They ordered from a small Korean kid who could not have been more than twelve.

"Isn't that illegal?" Eddie said, pointing at the kid.

"Kids are okay," Vaughn said. "They do stuff we don't know about. But they miss some stuff. So what?"

"Bob Dylan," Greta said.

"A famous case," Vaughn said. "I used to wonder about my father, why the things I talked about weren't interesting to him. I thought he didn't get it, but later I figured out he'd already been there and gone."

"It's generations," Eddie said. "Stuff gets squeezed down, dribbled out in pieces, leaving out half the shit."

"You lose the thought," Vaughn said.

"Pass the ketchup," Greta said. She was fixing her hamburger, decorating it with the condiments available. She did a grid pattern with the ketchup, which was in a red squeeze bottle with a good pointy tip.

"How did you know you could get a hamburger?" Eddie said.

"On the menu," she said. "Let me have that Chinese mustard, will you?"

Eddie pushed the pot of mustard her way. "I try to be friendly," he said. "Not kill people. That's worth doing. It's hard though."

"You're angry all the time," Greta said.

"Well, people are always doing stupid crap all over the place. I'd be a great guy if it weren't for other people."

"Eddie hates everybody equally," she said. She opened wide to bite the hamburger.

Vaughn stood the tiny cobs of corn that had come in his vegetable lo mein up on end at the edge of his plate and put other little cobs across the tops.

"Cornhenge," she said, nodding at his plate, her mouth full.

"Exactly," Vaughn said. "But I don't want to hate everybody. It's kind of, you know, ungenerous. And I don't like that. I want to like everybody."

"I like artists," Eddie said.

"You should make paintings," Greta said.

"I used to make paintings," Vaughn said. "I can't remember how anymore."

"I like thunder," Eddie said.

Greta made a face and did kidlike explosion sounds. "Thunder knocks me out. I like thunder better than lightning."

"Me, too," Eddie said.

"I stop what I'm doing and listen," she said. "I don't know anything about it, though. How it works or anything."

"I saw a show about thunder," Vaughn said. "I could tell you."

"You going to eat those little corn thingies?" Greta said.

"Knock yourself out," Vaughn said, carefully turning the plate so that the miniature corn cobs did not fall but ended up nearest her.

"Thanks," she said.

He watched Greta destroy the miniature structures on his plate, carefully unburdening the pillars with her fingers. She was funny, she was deft. What was the problem, after all? What was wrong with *this*?

"I remember stuff," she said. "Guys I liked when I was young, nights by the fire, being sort of crippled there was so much love, frightened and excited, being touched, fingers along my cheek, the smell of a guy's hand, the look of his smile, his eyes."

"I don't want to hear it," Eddie said.

"Don't worry," she said. "It's mostly gone now. Mostly I've got longing. Could be worse."

Vaughn watched them. They got along fine. He thought she had the longing thing right, too. Longing was powerful and sweet, but not so sweet as the thing itself, whatever the thing was. Whatever it was, they were distanced from it. As they got older they lived an evaporated life. They were captives, now shoved back into the game by accident—the dead spouse, the divorce, a runaway husband or wife. They might have gotten there on their own, but more likely not. They were withdrawn and maybe afraid. And if not exactly afraid, then something else, resigned. They'd gotten older and given up immediate, sensory pleasures for the abiding ones—comfort, the warmth of rooms, the dog's smile, chairs sunk comfortably into, the routine, the television series, the books they could bear to read, the magazines in which they actually found the photographs interesting. Sometimes they were caught longing, thinking back to some boyfriend or girlfriend, some apartment or some day or night, some frozen dawn when they burned all the firewood, then burned the fur-

niture to keep warm. It was bad furniture. Burning it was fun.
They thought back to a loft in New York, a house in Berkeley
with tatami mats on the floors, somewhere in Colorado, or
Florida, or Miami. The man or woman in memory.

For Vaughn it was hard to imagine how he'd gotten from
twenty to nearly fifty. How he was this person when he had
been that person. As a college kid he had been a painter. Then
he had a breakdown and couldn't speak for six weeks. He
went to bars with people every night. They listened to Edith
Piaf on the jukebox. They drank beer. The others spoke; he
did not speak. He went back to his place, an apartment over
a store where he made big derivative paintings with whatever
he had—footprints, sayings, cutouts, spray paint, tree parts,
stuff nailed to the stretchers, lightbulbs, street garbage, Po-
laroids. He didn't speak (that was his memory of it) for six
weeks. He didn't know why he had this breakdown, and he
didn't remember the breakdown, just the fact of the breakdown. And the aftermath. He wasn't a bad-looking kid then,
though kind of scruffy. When he looked at pictures of himself
at that time he thought he looked a little haunted, attractively
haunted. He was interested in what he had been thinking then.
He was interested in how he looked, his shirt cuffs unbuttoned,
his hair long, his beard full, his eye sockets deep. He wondered what had happened to all the people who were around
in those days. All those conversations he had listened to—all
the ideas people had then about the world, about painting,
about what needed to be done, about what art was or might
be. The bar—the bar was called George, he remembered that.
The women were thin, all wry smiles and smoke. They wore
lipstick and bracelets and rings. They walked like champions.
They weren't the smartest women in the world, but in mem-

ory they were unusually pretty—tired, sloe-eyed, smoky. He remembered thinking he was kind of dead. He couldn't talk. People kept asking him things, kept trying to help him talk. He'd get a word or half a sentence, the beginning of something, but he could never say it. It wouldn't come. There were times as the days wore on when a few words would come to him, then a sentence. He couldn't imagine what it was like, just that it was. He could say I like this, I want that, move over there, see this light. He remembered the boots he wore, heavy boots that hit the hardwood floors. He made pictures by intuition, imagination, the feel of the thing, the way a moment sits in time. The weight of it, the heft of it. The truth of it. The sense of fullness. It was not different from other things in life that were true. The crack of a ball against a bat when the sound itself said it was the long ball. The moment when a bolt began to thread or a bottle cap settled into its groove. But how was this turned into knowledge? How were such things explained to people who wanted the world simple, who insisted on *understanding*?

"We're used to knowing how something works and thinking that how it works is what it means," Vaughn said. "But how it works is only how it works; what it means is a completely different area of inquiry."

"What?" Eddie said.

"Thunder," Vaughn said. "I was thinking about thunder."

Vaughn wanted to explain this to Greta, but he did not know where to begin; and he worried, quite properly, that he might struggle with the explanation, only to discover that she was there ahead of him, waiting, with a coffee and a tart.

6

Gail called at two A.M. They were asleep, Greta in her bedroom, Vaughn in the guest bedroom. He snored, she said,
when they first tried to sleep together, and she poked him
repeatedly until he woke up and moved back into *his* room.
Later she got up and closed the door between the rooms. Now
he bunked there nightly.

He struggled to get to the phone before it woke Greta, but
they got to their phones in their separate rooms at the same
time, their "hellos" echoing.

"Can you come over now?" Gail said. "I've got some trouble here."

"Are you hurt?" Greta said.

"Gail?" Vaughn said. "What happened? Are you okay?"

"He went nuts on me."

"Tony?" Greta said.

"Right," Gail said. "I can't deal with this alone, can you come? Police are here."

"Shit," Vaughn said. "We're coming."

"We're on our way," Greta said.

They didn't so much get dressed as carry clothes to the car with them. Jeans, belts, shirts. He got behind the wheel. Greta jumped into the SUV's passenger seat.

"Did she sound bad?" he said. "She sounded bad, didn't she?"

"Yes," Greta said.

"Why can't she just curl up and weep like everybody else?"

"You are such a doll," Greta said. She was tying her shoes, the balls of her feet cocked on the dash.

They got to the beach highway and turned left, heading up Kiln Road to Interstate 10. Because the bridge across the Bay St. Louis had been out since Katrina, they had to take the long way around—up to the interstate, east toward Gulfport, and down to where his old house was in Hidden Lake. It was somewhat inland in a good section of the coast where the trees were old and gracious, the pine straw gently raked, the garages always closed, automatically. He and Gail had bought the house in higher times, when he was working for a developer, making a decent salary that was just begging to be spent on what was then an expensive quarter-million-dollar house. He thought at the time that it was above his pay grade, but Gail said everyone bought houses they couldn't quite afford. It was recommended. That worked fine until the bottom dropped out of the local market for upscale housing and Parsons, his boss at Parsons Development, turned out to have a unique idea about bookkeeping. Then the job went south and Vaughn never quite got it back together.

It took them nearly thirty minutes going the long way around. The house was brick and all lit up. There were five police cars, all of them with lights swirling and sifting across the neighbors' windows, striping the trees, lighting up the place like a gas station. They pulled into the driveway and found themselves with an eyeful of flashlight beam.

"Who're you?" the cop said.

"Husband," Vaughn said. "Is she all right? What happened?"

"I.D.?" cop said.

Vaughn plucked out his wallet and got his driver's license. The cop skated his light over the license, then back at Vaughn, then back to the license. "Looks like you. This address, yeah?"

"That's right," he said. "Used to be. Can we go in?"

Cop backed away from the car. "Who's the lady?"

"Her sister," Greta said.

The cop grabbed the walkie-talkie clipped to his shoulder and said, "Got the husband coming in with a friend." Then he flicked the light at Vaughn's waist. "Get your pants fixed, hey?" he said.

Gail was in the living room on one of the couches. She was crying and looked as if she'd been at it for a while. They had her stretched out and she looked lousy. She'd been hit hard and often, her face covered with bruises, scratches, cuts, and blood. Her lip was bloodied and blown up to the size of an oyster. There were cuts all over her face, neck, shoulders, and arms. Her hands were cut up—*defensive wounds,* he thought instantly, unable to stifle the TV cop show training. A large bruise was crowding one eye, shutting it down the way boxers get their eyes shut, tilted and squeezed. Her hair was matted and shot out to the side as if somebody was still pulling on it. There were veils of blood on her shoulder, down her upper arms, and there was part of a torn white shirt soaked in the blood. Other than the shirt and an ice pack, she was pretty much naked except for a beach towel printed like an American flag that he'd bought as a joke one time. Some cop had thrown his leather jacket into the mix, too.

Vaughn sat on the coffee table in front of the couch. Greta stayed above and behind Gail, almost as if to stay out of her line of sight.

"Hey," he said, reaching to move a twist of hair that was crossing the corner of her good eye. "What the fuck?"

"He is not as well mannered as some," Gail said, rolling her head back and up to look at Greta, who immediately moved around in front of the sofa and stood alongside Vaughn. "We were getting along fine until, you know, like . . . an argument. He said I was going to fuck around on him, he just knew it."

"You're going to get that with a guy who writes on your neck," Vaughn said. "What, he's fifteen?"

"Don't do that," Greta said, punching his shoulder. "Quit."

"What are you doing with a kid like this, Gail?" he said. "Is this all of it, the face? Hit you in the stomach, chest, anyplace?"

"Yeah, there's more, but the cop girl already looked me over. They got some other call, so somebody else is coming. I've got to have tests."

"So where is the little weasel? They get him?"

"No. He moved along. I don't want to fuck him over. He's just a kid."

"You're a sweetheart," Vaughn said. "What, like . . . what? Twenty?"

"Something," Gail said.

She kept crying in spurts and then one of the ambulance people walked him out the back door while the other EMTs took care of Gail, got her into the ambulance. The house had a glow to it, as ever. It was on a small lake, maybe twenty, thirty acres, houses all around, all built by Parsons before Vaughn had worked for him. It was pretty out on the deck in the evening, having the open lake between neighbors.

A few minutes more and they followed Gail to the hospital, the ambulance with its lights going a mile a minute but no siren, making for a smooth, quiet drive.

7

The hospital looked like a concert hall or a massive UFO that had landed and was lit up on the outside. It was designed by one of the casino architects who had seen too much Gehry and had been reading the magazines too hard. Various pieces of fine architecture of the moment had been cribbed into the Dinkelheim Memorial Hospital, the entrance to which they had some difficulty finding. Inside, it was the same old grubby hospital, just like any other hospital in any small town—or large town for that matter—in the country. It was a mess. The emergency room had cops and plastic curtains and alcoves where people took information from patients and twenty young people in colorful scrubs—this one taking your temperature, that one checking your Social Security number, the next one walking you to a curtained room in the next hall. They came in waves. Greta and Vaughn kept getting shunted out of one room after another, then called back in. The workers looked like department store clerks, checkers at grocery stores, wait staff at the local eateries. But here they had bright clothing and were all business. Greta and Vaughn spent some minutes trying to decide what color scrubs they liked best. Lime and lavender were winners.

Gail's wounds, in the fluorescents of the hospital, looked worse.

People came in to take her blood pressure, to ask questions, to move her from one room to the next, to do some small amount of probing, to change her from her American flag towel and torn shirt to a hospital gown. The cop's jacket was already gone. All the while he and Greta looked on and made all the jokes they could think of as quickly as they could make them. Gail had stopped crying. She rubbed at her neck as if to remove the name of her assailant, but the name would not budge.

It took some time but eventually she was settled in a room upstairs, tucked in for the night safe and sound, a room that was nice. A room Vaughn envied her, because it was quiet and clean and had lots of apparatus—machines behind the bed, metal plates on the wall, coiled black tubes and things with dials on them—and the doors to the closet and bath were an attractive light wood—maple, he thought—and there was a usable loveseat covered in a nubby fabric. The furnishings were Knoll. The room had a kind of reassuring chill, like a motel with extra sauce; but, of course, he wasn't staying.

Greta had come up in the elevator with him, then decided to make herself scarce and told him she'd meet him downstairs. He stayed with Gail for a bit in the room with the lights low and the hum of the air conditioner comforting, and he held her hand at the edge of the bed; and she stared at the television mounted near the ceiling and said, "Maybe you guys could come over and stay at the house a bit. Just a week or something. A couple weeks, maybe. I don't have this divorce thing quite together, really."

He squeezed her hand and made some kind of sound, just an utterance, a noise to indicate he'd heard.

"I know, it's odd, Vaughn, but here we are and I'm still having trouble. I was just so used to having you around, you know, being together even if it wasn't so great. And, I don't know, people aren't so interesting, maybe. Not that you're all that, but—"

"You really know how to treat a girl," he said.

"C'mon. It's not you anyway, it's everybody. Newton's always good. And I miss your father—all those sicko phone calls when he was sort of propositioning me? That was something. Remember that? After your mother died? He was in a bad way then."

"He was," Vaughn said.

"I wouldn't mind talking to him tonight," Gail said, picking up Vaughn's hand and dropping it back on the bed.

"I wouldn't mind talking to him either," Vaughn said.

She patted his hand. "Yeah, I know. Has that gotten any better?"

"Not really," he said. "I have to go in a minute."

"Maybe I'll call Newton. What time is it out there? Is it, like, midnight?"

"More like three-something," he said.

"Wake him up," she said.

The nurse who came to check up on Gail was very crisp. She walked well. Her skirt made a percussive sound, very quiet but insistent, like Tony Williams. The nurse was charming and friendly; she had a light laugh. Just the kind of woman Vaughn would want to check on him in the middle of the night after he'd gotten hammered in a car accident or a fistfight. He wondered why wives didn't do more checking on husbands in the middle of the night. Gail had never checked on him in the middle of the night. Greta never checked on him. Why? Probably in cowboy times the women all checked in on their cowboy husbands, because the women had some sense that they depended on those cowboy husbands, and that their relationships were predicated on a balanced distribution of duties and responsibilities, and that among the responsibilities of the women was checking on their cowboy husbands in the wee hours, just to be sure they had not been scalped by savages or mishandled by some disgruntled wranglers. Vaughn made a note to himself to bring this up to Greta later. He knew what she would say. She would say, "How do you know I don't check up on you?"

When the nurse was gone Gail said, "Okay, forget I mentioned the move thing. I'm doing fine. Just a little hiccup."

He leaned over the bed and kissed her on the cheek and felt how soft and lovely her skin was. He took in her scent as well, which, in spite of the mess of the evening, was not erased. It wasn't a scent he recognized from their marriage. It was the new scent she had been wearing *since* the marriage. It was a scent he found stirring, even seductive, in spite of everything.

Greta and Vaughn stopped at a green BP station to fill up the car and to get Greta some M&M's and Fritos, which, eaten together, "were sublime," she said. This was a specialty she'd picked up from her late husband. Then, Greta at the wheel, they were tooling down the beach highway stuffing their faces with M&M's and handfuls of corn chips.

He said, "She wants us to move over there."

"She does?" Greta said.

"Just for a bit. Just until things settle down."

"Wants *us* to move?"

"That's what she said."

"Fancy that," Greta said.

They rode in silence, the only sounds the tires rolling and the Fritos crunching. After a minute Vaughn said, "We don't have to do it. We could say no."

"You could say no," she said.

"Sure," he said. "I guess."

"I don't think so," Greta said. "I'm guessing this is a command performance and we're locked in."

"Might be that," he said.

"I don't mind," she said. "It's odd, but what isn't these days? Last time I talked to her, Gail asked if you were still going on about your father. I said you were."

"What a world," Vaughn said. "My ex and my new girl-friend discussing my problem with my father."

"It's not a problem," she said. "He's dead."

"It's a problem for me," Vaughn said. "I didn't do his death well."

"So you say. I told you it wasn't your fault."

"Not my fault he died or not my fault I wasn't good to him?"

"You loved him," she said. "Gail told me that. Told me all about the funeral, the telephone, the woman you had looking after him."

"There wasn't any funeral," he said.

"I know."

"I dispatched him over the phone. Into a cardboard box, into the fire."

"It's not the old way, but it's okay," Greta said. "It's modern."

"It was easy," he said. "That's what I noticed."

"You could have made a big deal out of it. Would that have been better?"

"Hey," he said. "Maybe it's fine to dump your old man over the phone with some funeral home weasel who gets prickly when he figures out you're going minimal on the arrangements."

"Gail said your father would have approved," Greta said.

"She's probably right," he said. "But there's me, too. I had him picked up at the house and shuttled to this joint where they burned what was left of him and blew the ashes out the back end of the oven."

"Now you're being dramatic."

"I didn't want to see him. I just wanted it over. I mean, once he was dead."

"Let's talk about something else," Greta said.

"You'd do more for a dog," he said.

"You're whining, Vaughn."

"Put him out for the garbage man," he said. "In that stupid white shirt and those stupid gray slacks he always wore."

Greta wiggled the steering wheel. "If you keep this up I'm going to crash and accidentally kill you."

"Okay," he said. He opened a second bag of M&M's. "Let's forget it."

He counted the M&M's in his palm. He added three Fritos. One of the Fritos was two Fritos stuck together. He popped the batch into his mouth. "You and Gail are more friendly than necessary," he said, munching.

"It's the modern world, blasted into the heart of your life," Greta said. "You're in the crosshairs of destiny."

"It might be better if you kept things on an ex-wife/new girlfriend basis?" His voice went up at the end so that she would be sure to get the question, so that she would be sure to understand that he was asking a question, not making an assertion.

"We're fine. We're just sort of half-friends," she said.

"Some things are between you and me, I mean."

"Duh," she said. "And some things are you and her."

"I didn't mean that," he said.

"Sure you did. That's cool," she said. "I'm not that into her."

"Whatever," he said, pinching a half-dozen Fritos in one hand, putting them in his mouth, then pouring a handful of M&M's. When he got the chewing down to something manageable he said, "I didn't take care of my father and then he died. That's the trouble. I think that's the trouble."

"Here we go," she said.

"We're responsible. Me and Newton. We didn't love him enough."

"Get out the love meter, baby."

"We never went over there. We called and pretended to care, but mostly we just waited to get off the phone. Maybe it was just me. I don't know what Newton did. Newton's just like him anyway."

"Newton is just like him?" she said.

Greta pulled the car off the road onto a sandy parking area that was used by beachgoers, shut off the lights, and ran the car windows down. It was muggy and a little chilly. They listened to the water of the Mississippi Sound slap around in the shallow bay. The stars were bright in the sky; there was a moon way off in the west. In one of the few houses across the street from the water someone was pulling an all-nighter, listening to an opera. Vaughn recognized an aria by some famous soprano; they heard bits and pieces of it over the sounds of the few cars running the coast highway that early in the morning.

Greta turned in the seat and said, "You loved him plenty, Vaughn. I don't know you that well, but I know you well enough to know that. You love him still. You feel guilty because he's dead, but you didn't do it. You have to understand, you have to kind of get serious about this, because it becomes a problem after a while. One way or another everybody fucks up sometime. So even if you did fuck up, which I can't figure, it's over now."

"In a big way," he said.

"Oh, please," she said. She danced in her seat, arms in the air. "Drama queen, drama queen."

"Am not," he said. "We weren't kind and then he *died*."

"I don't want to play this," she said. "He died because it was time. He was old. Your mother died a year before or something, whatever it was. Did you kill her, too?"

"No. But everybody loved her. She was an angel. She was the Little Town of Bethlehem. She was St. Theresa of the Little Flower, whatever her name was, only she wasn't little."

"A medium-sized flower then," Greta said.

"Ha ha ha ha," he said.

"Sorry," she said. "You were fine with your mother's death,

but you believe you contributed to your father's death. I don't know. I've only known you what, four months? Five? Already I've heard enough about this."

"He was sort of annoying," Vaughn said. "I mean, he wasn't annoying that last year—he was just sort of pitiful—but before that he'd been annoying. I mean like when both of them were alive. And when we were children, he was annoying."

"Not unusual," she said.

"We never really hugged him once we were adults," he said.

"Oh God, hugging," she said. "Too much. Call Oprah. Where are the M&M's?"

He handed her the bag. It was getting light in the east. He liked sitting out there by the beach listening to the sounds, looking at the lights. The early morning was lovely, the sounds were soothing and constant—the hiss of car tires, the light splash of the water in the gulf, the crickets, the buzzing electronics of the streetlights. Very musical.

After a few minutes he said, "Okay. Here's the deal. I'll get over it. But I feel this and I'm not going to stop feeling it because you say it's silly, or you say I did fine. I did not pay enough attention to my father. I didn't call him. I didn't go see him. I didn't take care of him. I didn't respond to hints he made in conversation. I think he wanted to come live with us. I knew it but I ignored it. When it came up, I'd say, 'Well, that's an idea. We can think about that.' I was trying to get him into a home where people would take care of him, other people, where he would pay people to see to his needs, really to be friends. But of course, the people in those places aren't very often friends, are they? And we knew that, Newton and I. We went over there and tried to get him

58

interested in the idea—took him around, showed him various old folks' homes where he could buy a crummy future. We almost had him convinced once. It wasn't a bad place. Some of the places were frightening, but a couple were livable. One was kind of charming, like a bigger version of a good hospital room. It had that kind of hospital room feel about it, but it would have been just that room, a single room, all the time. He would have to go out in the hall to meet anybody, to see any of the other people. The hall was like the street. He'd have this room instead of an apartment or a house. In fact, I think Newton looked at an apartment one time. Newton the Fancy, the Swell, the Well-to-Do. I should tell you about Newton someday."

"You've told me already," she said. "You don't like him."

"I like him well enough. I used to, anyway," he said. "He's my brother. I love him. I care for him."

"No, you don't," she said. "You wouldn't kill your father, but your brother, maybe."

"Where do you get these ideas?" he said.

"Double duh," she said.

"Okay, he's sort of a jerk. I'll give you that. I'll just admit that right up front. He's full of himself. He's thrilled to be alive and he thinks the world should be thrilled right along with him. He's condescending, presumptuous, controlling, devious, self-centered, and narcissistic."

"Hey! Welcome home!"

"I know," he said. "Everyone in my family. Well, everyone but my mother. She was none of that."

"Your brother is very successful," Greta said. "This upsets you."

"Of course it does. Everybody loves him."

"If everybody hated him, you'd be buddies, right?"

"Probably," he said.

"So you feel better now? Cleansed? Did you get this passion for truth and justice from your father? That sounds like your father. Everything I've heard about your father, that sounds like him, like what he wanted more than anything else."

"Well, he didn't get much from us, not the last days, anyway."

"How many days was it? Let's talk about this; let's get down to brass tacks. How many days?"

"Don't be funny," he said.

"I'm not being funny," she said. "Are you talking the last week or the last six weeks or the last hundred days? What? Six months?"

"From the moment my mother died until the day he died. A year and a half. But he was old. I mean, I'd written him off before that, but I think before that I was acting okay. It was after Mother died that I couldn't bear him anymore. He knew it, too. He knew as soon as she was gone it was all over for him. He knew that we'd only been paying as much attention to him as we had been for her sake. That's probably the worst of it."

"That's bad," Greta said. "That couldn't have been much fun for him."

"Exactly," Vaughn said.

Some geese were flying by and honking. Vaughn looked up in the sky—he couldn't see them. There were a lot of lights up and down the highway along the edge of the water but no geese that he could see. They were odd-sounding.

Greta started the car. "Let's go to the house," she said. "I'm tired."

"Me, too," he said. "This is weird shit with Gail, huh? I feel better having said this stuff. I don't know. Who knows what's happening next?"

"What do you mean?"

"Moving," he said.

They had started rolling out of the car park, tires crunching the sand, and the car stopped suddenly. Greta turned to him and said, "It's fine. Just don't make a big deal out of it."

"Okay," he said.

"I don't *want* to do it," she said. "But it's not a deal killer. Eddie can take care of the house. We can stay over there. Or you could, for that matter. I don't have to, if Gail would rather."

"No," Vaughn said. "She said 'us' specifically. 'Us' is what she said. I said I'd talk to you about it."

"It is kind of crazy," Greta said. "Your house, your ex-wife—nutball."

"I could tell her you said no."

"Great," Greta said. "No, thanks. It's a short-term thing anyway, just to get her straightened away."

"She was pretty beat up," he said.

"We didn't do it, Vaughn."

"We are angels of mercy," he said.

"Oh Jesus," she said.

8

Back at Greta's he couldn't sleep. The morning sun was glowing in the smeary windows and neighbors were moving around outside, chain saws chattered, tiny rented bulldozers roared. The guest bedroom was too small, too cluttered, and Vaughn felt out of place, and he was worried about Gail. He lay in the bed holding his eyes shut with his fingertips and thought about the thoughts running through his brain, which were mostly about his father, who was dead, and about whom he thought more often than ever. This morning he imagined, as he often did, his father's life during the year after his mother died. His father lived then in the two-bedroom, two-story apartment outside Atlanta in the group of four hundred apartments called the Mark V that he and Vaughn's mother picked out years before—a large apartment in a gated development with landscaped lawns, large sections of glass in the buildings, brick construction, shingled roofs, handsome fences around the patios, small private gardens.

His father had the corner apartment, and he was alone now all the time except for when the woman came in from Catholic Services. This was a woman Vaughn had hired when his father started using the walker—an aluminum apparatus with wheels on the front, feet to the back. He also had a wheelchair, which Vaughn had bought for him.

The woman who came in every day to care for Vaughn's father arrived at eight o'clock in the morning. She cleaned up, made him breakfast, turned on the television—for him at first, and then, when he got tired, for herself, the Spanish stations, the volume very low. Often Vaughn's father did not know her name since the same woman did not come every day. Usually there were two different women every week. Sometimes the same two women for two weeks, then two other women the next two weeks. Sometimes three women a week. It was never the same. It went on like that. None of them spoke English well. Vaughn's father spoke no Spanish. He was an orderly man and kept the apartment clean with the help of these women. He had all of his important papers and documents lined up on the dining room table in stacks. When he looked for his investments, he knew exactly where they were, in which folders, in which stacks. Insurance, similarly. Medical papers, the same—all arranged around the dining table so he could get at them as necessary. At one end of the table were his personal items—his car keys, though he hadn't driven in over a year, his wallet, change, the credit cards he gave to the women when they went to the grocery store for him. He had recently stopped going upstairs because the stairs were impossible. There had been talk about renting a new apartment all on one floor, but moving seemed out of the question, so he had abandoned the upstairs of the town house. He lived downstairs—the kitchen, the living room, a small bath, the dining area, a small den. The living room was large and open, with a nine-foot ceiling and white, cut-pile carpet, white walls, white vertical blinds covering a pair of three-panel sliding glass doors on the west wall. Outside, a small patio was surrounded by fencing on which still grew a vine he had planted many years before. The vine seemed lavish—lacy green stems dotted with pretty pink flowers.

When the woman who was taking care of him arrived, she opened the blinds and flooded the downstairs of the apartment with light. Because the weather had already turned cool, she opened the sliding doors to air out the apartment. Vaughn's father was still resting on the couch in his blue pajamas, his body tangled in sheets. The sheets were not fitted to the couch, of course, but he was short and it was a large couch, so he fit inside its arms. It was the size of a coffin. Every night he slept there on top of a sheet with a second flat sheet pulled over him, and often a blanket in winter. The woman had a Catholic Services name tag on her uniform. He dozed off after the woman arrived, then woke again with a start to the smell of bacon and eggs, elbowed himself up on the couch, and slid into his wheelchair, rolled himself over to the bathroom, and backed into it so he could relieve himself. He missed the bowl as he did almost every morning. He wanted to pee sitting down on the toilet, but he couldn't, so he struggled to his feet holding on to the vanity on his left, and a handle on the wall to his right that had been placed there for him. Still, he missed the bowl.

He called to the woman in the kitchen, and when she came out and knocked on the bathroom door, he asked her to help clean him up with a washcloth that he handed her. She rinsed it in the sink, soaped it lightly, stripped off his shirt and cleaned his armpits, his chest, his shoulders, his arms, his wrists, his hands. She cleaned his neck and his back, rinsing with a barely damp cloth. He watched all this in the bathroom mirror. The woman was not unattractive. She was young and dark-skinned and wore an odd-colored lipstick, something in the flaming-brick range. She washed his face with the wash-cloth, taking special care around his eyes, his ears, under his chin, at the back of his neck.

"You have to clean down there," he said, pointing.

She pointed, too, and raised her eyebrows. He nodded. She turned to the sink and rinsed the washcloth again.

"Take the trousers off," he said, motioning to his waistband. He was facing her. She hooked her forefingers in the waist-band on either side and pulled the pants down to his ankles. She went all the way to the carpet with the pajama pants, squatting there, holding the waistband at the floor.

"Help me get my feet out," he said, slapping his leg and motioning upward with his hand. She remained crouched there, lifting first his left foot by the ankle, then his right, and snapping the pajama pants out from under each foot in turn. Now he stood there naked in the small bathroom with the woman from Catholic Services, who retrieved the washcloth from the edge of the lavatory and began to clean his penis and his testicles, to rinse his pubic hair, to wipe between his legs with the washcloth, to clean his backside and the crack of his ass, constantly rinsing the washcloth, soaping it lightly, ap-plying the soap, then re-rinsing and applying the damp cloth to his skin. In this way she worked down his legs to his feet, cleaning the tops and then, as if he were a plump two-legged horse, lifting one leg after another, and reaching around to clean the bottoms of his feet.

When she had cleaned him head-to-toe, she said, "You dirty," and motioned with her hand for him to stand there and allow the air to dry him while she took the washcloth and the pajamas into the laundry area in the kitchen.

Vaughn's father stared at himself in the bathroom mirror. He reached down and encircled the head of his penis with his thumb and forefinger and pulled the penis out and down, as if trying to elongate his member, to un-shrivel it, but the penis would not cooperate and it contracted back into the extra flesh and hair of his crotch. It was barely there at all.

When the woman returned she had fresh pajamas—white this time, with blue piping—folded over her arm. She shook out the pants and put them on the white carpeted floor of the bathroom, like two small connected pools, and then in the reverse of the procedure used to take off his pajama pants, she put one foot after the other in a leg hole, and then pulled the pants up and knotted them at his waist and tied a bow there. She held out the pajama top as if helping a gentleman on with his coat and threaded his left arm, then his right into the sleeves, and then returned to the front and buttoned him up—four buttons—bottom to top. She patted his arm and smiled at him, wiggled her finger in a circle to tell him to turn around and face away from the bathroom door, then fetched the wheelchair, which had been around the corner, just outside the bathroom, the whole time. She rolled the chair up behind him, helped him sit, and pulled him backward out of the bathroom and into the living room where she pushed him to the small table at which he would eat the breakfast she had been keeping warm on a hot plate in the kitchen.

As he was eating, and knowing that she could not understand what he said, he spoke to her, while she was in the kitchen cleaning up.

"I expect to hear from the boys today," he said. "I expect to get a couple of calls today. We have some business to talk over—some matters about the estate." He ate his eggs—they were poached—and his toast, and he listened to himself chew, and he looked out the window at the little pink flowers crawling on the wooden fence of the patio.

Speaking louder, he said, "I'm going to need you to go to the store for me today."

She turned around and said, *"Qué?"*

"The store," he said. *"Groceria."*

"Sí," she said.

"I'll need to make a list," he said.

"Qué?" she said again from the kitchen.

"I'll give you a credit card," he said.

"Card," the woman said.

"I think I'm going to need some things from the store," he said again, and this time she did not reply.

At mid-morning he busied himself with a grocery list. He worked first from memory, then rolled into the kitchen and opened the cabinets, one after another, with a rubber-tipped stick that he had made for this purpose. He had the Catholic Services women front all the cans in the cabinets so he could see what vegetables he had in those cans, so that he could inventory his holdings in vegetables. If there was a blank spot at the front of a shelf, he knew he needed peas, beans, or soup, depending upon which row was empty. He was an orderly man.

At noon he gave her the list, gave her the keys to the car, and gave her his Visa card along with a signature card that she needed to show at the grocery store so that she could sign the Visa receipt.

At the door she turned and said, "Chips? You want chips?"

He shook his head. "No, we have chips." He waved at her from across the room. She went out and he listened to the door lock.

When she was gone, he returned to the bathroom and with an elaborate effort managed to get himself out of the wheel-chair and onto the toilet. This was such a relief for him, to be sitting on the toilet. He sighed and closed his eyes, grateful to be alone in the house and to be in the bathroom with his stick, the one he used in the kitchen and elsewhere when there were things out of reach that needed to be touched or moved. Now he used the stick, reaching out toward the door and shoving it almost closed. Now he waited.

Minutes passed, a quarter hour. He wanted to go to the toilet now, because if he could, then the woman would, if necessary, clean him up when she returned. If he didn't go to the toilet now and he had to go after she left for the evening, there would be no one to clean him up. He could do it himself with the toilet paper, but the results were not always satis-factory. He could do it with the washcloth, but that required cleaning the washcloth, and sometimes the sink and vanity, and the results were often not completely satisfactory. He preferred when the girl did it, though while he was there on the toilet in the small bathroom, he noted with comfort that there were dozens of washcloths folded and stacked alongside the lavatory.

On this occasion he managed to shit and on inspection saw that the shit was well-formed, well-colored, and cleanly off him. Buoyed by his success, he wiped his bottom several times with the toilet paper, flushing the toilet after each pass, and then, without getting off the toilet, wet a washcloth and passed the wet cloth between his legs. It burned his skin but after a couple of attempts the cloth emerged unsoiled, and he returned it to the sink, under the running water. He pulled up his pajama pants, and eventually got back into the wheelchair, rinsed the washcloth, then got out of the bathroom, and back into the living room where he sat in the wheelchair facing the couch where he slept every night, realizing that the sheets were not freshly folded on the arm of the couch where they usually were with most of the other Catholic Services women who saw to him.

Later in the afternoon he watched CNN as the woman prepared his lunch—a small, bony steak. In the news that day: a drive-by shooting in Los Angeles, more casualties in a recent airliner crash, a rise in the snake population of Alaska. When he switched to the local weather channel, he saw that rain was expected by the end of the week. His testicles itched.

As the afternoon dragged on he took a nap, and the woman retreated to the kitchen where she turned up the volume on her TV, a nine-inch model he had bought especially for the Catholic Services women, and which was connected to the cable service that provided two dozen Spanish-language channels. At five-thirty she put his dinner on the TV tray and then she was out the door, smiling. He gave her a thumbs-up and a nod, and when the door closed he lifted the plastic top she had put over his plate, surveyed the food, and then replaced the top. "Too early to eat," he said, to no one.

In the early evening Vaughn's father telephoned Vaughn's wife, Gail. This was before the divorce, although there was already talk of it, and Vaughn's father was party to that talk. He found her at home and talked to her for some time about how much he missed her and about how much he missed the old times when she and Vaughn would come to visit. He told her he had a particular fondness for her and that she was always his favorite of his sons' wives. He wished she would come visit him sometime. He needed someone to take care of him, someone with whom he could talk, with whom he might share a meal, an evening. She was welcome to stay at the apartment. In fact, he would like it if she would stay at the apartment. It would remind him of old times.

She said that might be a little iffy.

"Nonsense," he said. "Not at all. In fact, if you get tired of my son, you can come and live with me. And by the way, how is your job going?"

"Fine," she said.

"Maybe you could divorce my son, quit your job, and come and live with me," he said. "I could provide for you."

"We aren't divorced yet," she said to Vaughn's father. "No matter what you think."

Vaughn's father, who was eighty-six, fell silent. Gail, who had presented herself to him as, perhaps truthfully, as sweet a woman as ever walked this earth, said, "Maybe later I could.

Maybe I could come live there with you and take care of you. I could cook and do that sort of thing."

"It might not be too bad," Vaughn's father said. "You don't really have a husband, do you?"

"Well, sort of," she said, and they laughed together.

They went on talking about this as if it were a real possibility. Later she would report to Vaughn that on many occasions his father offered to do his best to satisfy her in every possible way.

That night Vaughn's father watched a football game on television. He moved from the wheelchair to one of the deep, soft easy chairs that he and Vaughn's mother used to sit in every night when they watched television. He still sat in his chair while his wife's chair, a little tattered, remained empty. He watched the football game for a while with the sound on, barely following the action. The sound was loud as it ricocheted around the room, and he found that comforting. Later he turned off the sound and stared at the game and past the game to the brightly colored jerseys, the screaming green field, the bright lights, the fans, the players and their sparkling helmets. He stared and wondered what would become of him, how he would go on living alone in the apartment. Eventually he was just staring at the wall off to one side of the television, barely aware of the movement on the screen, a shadow-play in his peripheral vision. By eleven he was asleep in the chair. The food was untouched on the TV tray; the television was running. All the lights downstairs were on. Outside, footsteps of the other apartment dwellers passed back and forth in front of his door. In the distance trucks could be heard gearing up and gearing down on the freeway heading out of town. Air-conditioning compressors clicked on and off. Crickets sang. The night rolled on.

He awakened at three-thirty in the morning, disoriented, and he stayed in his chair for a minute trying to get his bearings. The television was showing some kind of sports news program with two young anchorpeople. The TV tray was just out of reach in front of him and to the left, on the other side of his chair. The covered plate was still on the tray, along with a glass of water with condensation on the sides. There was silverware there. After a few moments in the easy chair, he sat up and pulled the wheelchair to him and began to transfer himself into the wheelchair so that he could go to the bathroom. He managed to get into the chair and to the bathroom, where he missed the bowl.

Coming out, he decided to try the walker. It was chilly in the apartment and he wanted to look at some papers on the table, and to close the curtains. He did these things successfully, using the walker. He wondered why no one ever called him—why Vaughn did not call him, why Newton did not call him. He wondered why he had to live there alone, tended by a woman who didn't speak English, and who changed day by day. He wondered where his friends were, where his family was. He wondered what he had done to earn himself this precarious and uncomfortable circumstance. He remembered when he was a powerful man, successful, well-regarded, a leader of other men and the prince of his family.

He remembered his wife and the fight they had the night she fell in the den and hit her head on the coffee table and how that started her sudden speedy decline. He wished they had not had the argument; it was about something silly. They had been together for so long and had had so many arguments that every new one seemed to be about life and death. He wondered whether, if she had not fallen, she would be alive and there with him still. He regretted treating his wife badly in the final years of their marriage, regretted that he was unable to cope with her problems and his own problems and the loss of authority, the loss of purchase in the world, the sense that both of them were lost in time and space and that she was no longer any good to him in the way she had been previously, and that it didn't matter anyway since he was worthless himself. The children, the two sons, had loved her immensely and in her decline had been with her constantly. They traveled to town and stayed with her at the hospital, stayed with her at the rest home even when she could not speak, and when she was comatose they had stayed by her side. Days and days and weeks, on into months, when finally at his insistence the feeding tube was removed from her stomach, and his wife and their mother passed on within days. He wondered if that was why they had forsaken him, or was it more? Was it everything that he did and did not do—the whole of his performance, every slight, every strong word, every missed expression of affection, attention not showered? Was it everything? He did not have an answer.

He sat in his apartment in his wheelchair. The television was blinking in the other room, and he sat in the middle of the living room and he did not know. He was tired and dizzy, sick to his stomach. Suddenly his head jerked and it felt as though someone had hit him with a bat, but no one had hit him. Everything swam in front of him, and he thought he should lie down. He got out of the wheelchair and reached for the walker, but missed and stumbled onto the couch, his legs splayed under the coffee table, his powerful hands still locked on the aluminum handles of the wheelchair. He began to cry. There was nothing left to do. There was nothing he could do. He tried to get up and get under the sheet on the couch, but he was on top of the sheet and couldn't seem to lift himself off the sheet in order to get it out from under him and spread it over himself for sleeping. His legs were stiff and heavy, hard to move, like weights attached to his body. He couldn't move very well and he was dizzy and he closed his eyes and let his head fall forward onto the couch; he stayed that way for a few minutes, and then he was asleep again.

When the Catholic Services woman, a new woman that next day, arrived in the morning, she found him like that, one leg twisted under the coffee table, his head on the couch, his hands covering his head. She helped him up and onto the couch, where he rested, breathing heavily for a few minutes. She was worried and called the Catholic Services office to report, then checked him again and found that he was breathing smoothly and sleeping on his back on a rumpled sheet on the couch. She went to the kitchen to prepare breakfast. When she returned a few minutes later with eggs and toast and jam, he smiled at her and asked for help getting into the wheelchair. He said, "I have some things I want to get done later."

"*Qué?*" she said.

9

Gail was released from the hospital late the next day and she called Greta's house to thank them for their help and to report that she had gotten a cab back to the house and that she was fine. She wanted to talk to Greta, but Greta was out so Vaughn talked to her. She asked how he'd been and he said he was okay. He didn't want to talk to her because talking to her made him nervous; he didn't feel comfortable talking about anything.

"I want to file charges," he said. "I want you to."

"I don't know," Gail said.

"Come on, Gail. This is fucked."

"It is, but, you know, you're you and I'm me. It's a one-time thing."

"No way to know that," he said. "Even if it is, it's way beyond letting it go. I think we've got to do it."

"Let me think about it," she said. "Just get back a little. So . . . what are you doing these days, anyway?"

He was quiet a minute, then said, "Emergency housing. Tiny places you can build for not much and take to a site on the back of a truck. Assemble in a week."

"No kidding," she said. "Like those things they tried to sell at Lowe's after Katrina? Little carpenter gothic cottages?"

"Not really, no. More like in cool trailers, I guess. Except for the trailer part."

"I don't like trailers much," she said.

"I know," he said.

They talked like that for a few minutes, with lots of dead air growing between their lines of dialogue. Finally, Gail said, "I just wanted to check in, say thanks for everything. I'm doing better and I think things will get better from here."

"We live in hope," he said.

"I'll let you go. I'll call Greta later, catch up with her."

"Okay," he said. "We need to talk more."

"I know," she said.

Hanging up, he was thinking he had originally liked Gail because she was always disappointed in herself. You could hear it in her voice, a kind of deadness. It was like some people got it, and knew they'd failed, and others didn't get it at all. What was best was to know you were screwed and to be okay with that. The people he didn't like insisted on imagining themselves excellent and in good order.

Gail had been a basket case early in their marriage, always going up walls, making shit up, doing drugs, disappearing in the middle of the night and staying gone days at a time, calling him from a distant Wal-Mart at six in the morning to whisper that she was being followed, or busting out of the house on foot in the rain after an argument and calling from a pay phone in the bus station three hours later with two "friends" she couldn't seem to get rid of. That had been the pattern for a time. He got her to see a therapist who straightened her out, though after a year she started treating problems with platitudes, categorical ideas that clearly weren't hers. He tried, in their marriage, to make her feel loved, and sometimes he did love her intensely, he ached for her—*ached with tenderness* was the joke they made about it. She was the queen and he was the worker bee, scuttling around doing stuff for her. When she was lonely, he called people. When she was scattered, he put things in order. When she forgot, he reminded her. When she didn't understand, he explained. It got a little tiring. She went into rehab. And then to the therapist. After that she turned into somebody he didn't quite recognize, which he thought was heartbreaking.

It *was* heartbreaking. She was a little dull. He tried to be understanding. He figured she needed to be the way she was, that this was the price for normalizing her behavior. She needed flattery, she needed authority, she needed clarity, and it did not matter if these were poorly rooted. She became an NPR person, a reverse Stepford Wife, and every idea was canon, received over the airwaves, preached with fervor and charm, believed deeply, for the common good. A cigar-store liberal. Where before she was equal parts liberal, conservative, anarchist, hedonist, hair-puller, now she took positions about what could and could not be said about women, what jokes could and could not be told, what ideas could be countenanced and what ideas could not. That's where he had her, reminding her that all ideas could be countenanced. She knew that, didn't she? Every idea is just a scheme, a deployment of players and elements, a reflection on possibility.

Wrong. And then, finally, they were not on the same wavelength. They no longer raised their eyebrows at the same things, snickered together, or shook their heads at the same sights, remarks, or ideas. It was as if one of them suddenly *fit in the world* and the whole structure of their relationship collapsed. Call it what you might, the change divided them to a degree that they could not have imagined. They lived together like that way too long.

Eddie knocked on the back door, then opened it and let himself into the kitchen. He went straight to the refrigerator and got out a bottle of beer, removing the cap with his teeth. "What're you guys doing?" he said.

"I'm hanging around waiting for Greta," Vaughn said. "Gail's out of the hospital."

"Good for her." Eddie took a pull on the beer, then said, "They get the creep?"

"I don't think they're going to get anybody. Gail isn't going to give him up."

"Great. Why doesn't she just invite him back over, give him a sap or something. Jesus."

"I know."

"Shit," he said. "I just watched this war show. Fucking people are such fucks. Those old dudes who used to do television would never have put up with the shit they do now."

"What're you talking about?"

"Usual shit," Eddie said, bending over the sink to look out

into the backyard toward his garage apartment. "You know I can hardly remember a thing about what happened when the hand went? It was, like, all of a sudden there was mush on my arm."

"That's ugly," Vaughn said.

"Was," Eddie said. "But that was the name of the game, ugly. I used to keep news stories. I had a laptop. You could get stuff online—message boards, news service. It was pre-Internet, almost. But we had a lot of crap over there. Pictures—bodies, body parts, tinker-toys, bits and pieces of people, like that 'highway of death' thing. Guys were trading that shit like bubble-gum cards. And I got stories from guys, from all over, the shit we did, atrocities, torture, whatever. It was just like this new one. We can't run a war anymore. It's all kids and grotesque coaches."

"Now we *start* wars," Vaughn said.

"Yeah, that's probably new."

"And we're all driving to Wal-Mart with Support Our Troops ribbons magneted to the backs of our cars. Of course, every American is worth four thousand Iraqis. We're more human, I guess."

"Covered that already," Eddie said. "It's a fucking football game. Get over it."

"I'm thinking I loathe this country these days," Vaughn said.

"It's not what it was," Eddie said. "That's for sure."

"Maybe it'll get better," Vaughn said. "In the fullness of time."

Eddie held up his beer bottle for a toast and said, "Bad memories," and Vaughn banged his Coke can into the bottle and they drank to that.

"The good news is I don't remember much," Eddie said, looking at the handless arm. "Fucking memory doesn't work right. Shit happens and it's over and you're left with a before and after. It's crap. It barely even names the shit that happened—bomb, rocket attack, sandstorm. It's not a real full-color seven-channel surround-sound memory of the experience."

"Could be that's a blessing," Vaughn said.

"Maybe," Eddie said. "Maybe not. You want to go to the bar? I'm going."

"What, now?" Vaughn didn't want to go, but felt bad. He said, "I'm waiting here awhile. Maybe we'll come over later."

Eddie left out the back door, taking a fresh beer from the refrigerator on his way.

He was right about memory. Vaughn's was spotty. He and Gail had a car crash on the highway once, him driving, and that had stuck with him pretty clear for a year or so, so that at times the whole event would replay itself in his head, except it was very fast. A few seconds, maybe, from when he lost control of the car in the rain at seventy miles an hour, slid across the highway and down a twenty-foot embankment of wet grass and head-on into a ten-inch-diameter, forty-foot-tall pine. When that replayed itself the first year after it happened it was plenty clear, plenty vivid. But it stopped after a while.

He could not remember much about the first girl he ever slept with—not her name, what she looked like, what she felt like—next to nothing. It was on an aluminum chaise in her backyard. It had been raining. She had a lot of blond hair. The memories were just tokens, words, facts, nothing sensory. And he wasn't even sure she was the one, because he remembered another woman with red hair in an apartment—an attic apartment, it seemed like. The other girls from around that time were all similarly schematic in memory. A girl from architectural school who was from Louisiana. A girl he met at Mardi Gras in New Orleans—she was from West Texas, traveling with her mother in a white Cadillac. He was very drunk and had a cast on his arm. They picked him up in the French Quarter and took him to a motel out in Metairie. He went into the room and there were a dozen people sleeping there—mostly girls, in beds, on couches, on the floor—and the mother told him to sleep in the car. He was drunk and he did, but the girl came out and stayed with him for a while. She was faceless. How were you supposed to remember these things? What was the girl's name? She was pretty, he thought. He remembered her as pretty, though he had no memory of what she looked like.

Vaughn started cleaning up around Greta's place. He vacuumed the hardwood floor with a broom-vac, dusted some, restacked the magazines, picked up the dog's chew toys and put them in the wicker basket, and wiped the kitchen cabinets after he'd rinsed the dishes and put them in the new Bosch dishwasher that Greta was so proud of. It didn't have any dials on the face of it. The controls were on the top of the door, which closed up under the lip of the countertop.

Newton called and wondered how things were going. "What's up, Red?" he said. Sometimes Newton called him Red. It was a joke of their father's, about how people used to call their father Red when he was in college, when he had red hair.

"Nothing," Vaughn said. "You okay?"

"Sure am," Newton said. "I got a call from Gail. She's worried about you."

"The feeling's mutual. She tell you about her adventure?"

"Yessir," he said. "Chapter and verse. You and the new—what, companion?—to the rescue. Hospital nights. The whole story. Just like old times. Is she okay? She said she was okay."

"I haven't seen her since she got out," Vaughn said. "She was a mess when she went in. I've seen worse, but only in movies."

"She told me you were talking about our dad again."

"He came up. Actually, she brought him up."

"Yeah—the *proposition.* He was whacked to the end."

"Seemed so then," Vaughn said. "Doesn't seem so crazy now."

"Yeah it does," Newton said. "Really. So, anyway, uh—you need any help? Anything I can do?"

"We're fine," Vaughn said.

"Got any work?"

"No. Well, I'm messing with a few things. I have a couple ideas that might turn into something."

"Hmm," he said. "Is the place still a wreck? I saw some video and it looks like nothing's happening, like nobody's doing anything since the storm."

"That's just along the coast, here to Ocean Springs, parts of Pascagoula," Vaughn said. "Really just the beachfront. The rest is kind of normal. Full recovery is expected anytime now. Buildings—new casinos going in. They're going to try to make it more casino-centric."

"Bravo, Mississippi," Newton said. "Just what was needed."

"You could buy property down here," Vaughn said. "Lots available."

"Prices way too high," Newton said. "I checked."

"Ah."

"Gail says she's not quite worked out the single life. She said she asked you to move in over there. You going to do that?"

"Might. We talked about it, Greta and me. For a while, maybe a few weeks or something, help Gail out."

"Think it would?"

"I don't know. She's upset. This guy smacks her around and I don't know if that's the end of it or the first of many. So, yeah, we might do something."

At that moment Vaughn suddenly remembered Newton's first wife. Rita. She had a red nose. She had a lot of black hair. She wore wide print skirts, very colorful. She wore socks, white. She had a red, runny nose. She had watery eyes. Her eyes bulged out of her head. Newton told him she was very smart. She graduated from Rice, he said. She had big, red lips. Rheumy eyes. Her nose was running all the time. She would blow her nose and rub her nose, and it would get red. She sat with one leg crossed under her in the big modern chairs at the house.

"Well, call me if I can help," Newton said. "I mean, really."

"I will," Vaughn said. "If it spirals out of control, you'll be the first to know."

"Okay, Vaughn," he said. "So long."

Years ago, when Vaughn had talks with his father, they would sit in his father's office at the house and his father would explain things to him. It was very comfortable, and reassuring, because his father had the manner of a man who knew things, and thus Vaughn was protected. His father knew how things worked, and he told Vaughn how they worked; he explained the details, the motivations, the expectations, and the desires. At first, Vaughn was glad to get all this information, but later he resented it. He began to like his father less well, and thought his explanations lacked something in the way of subtlety, and had a curious self-aggrandizing aspect that Vaughn figured couldn't be healthy. Later still he felt sorry for his father, trapped in a life that required him to always be the hero.

When his father and mother moved into the apartment in Atlanta, they got on each other's nerves all the time, as when his father decided his mother should not take too much aspirin. They were in their eighties by then, and Vaughn's mother was in the habit of taking an aspirin every day. She may have been taking it to thin the blood, against the possibility of heart trouble—or maybe it was just to help her sleep, or for a headache she had—but in any case she would want to take one Bayer aspirin, just one, every evening, and after a time this upset his father. Vaughn never understood why. Perhaps it was her reliance on the pill. Perhaps his father thought it was some kind of pacifier, a weakness; but whatever the reason, her dependence on the aspirin upset him so much that he eventually hid the aspirin from her. He hid it in a box in the desk drawer in his home office so that she couldn't find the box; and once, when he was telling Vaughn about this, he showed Vaughn the box with the aspirin in it. He was grave about this hidden aspirin. He took Vaughn into his confidence and explained that Vaughn must never tell his mother where the aspirin were. Vaughn agreed to keep his father's secret, a promise that he kept. But he also went to the store and bought his mother two dozen small tins of Bayer aspirin that she could take to her heart's content.

Monkey came around and Vaughn thought the dog was looking to go outside, so he went to the door and opened it, but Monkey stayed where he was; and when Vaughn asked him, "You want to go outside?" and gestured out the door, Monkey got down on all fours. Vaughn took that to mean no, and went back to the couch.

He turned on the television and caught the last half of *Engineering Disasters 10,* which included the Tropicana Casino Garage Collapse, the Transvaal Aqua Park Roof Implosion, the Metternich & Steinke Gas Storage Explosion, and the Bhopal Chemical Plant Disaster. There were a lot of workers on this show, guys in greasy overalls and hard hats, guys with walkie-talkies, guys with big electrical control boxes with big black buttons on them. He envied these guys the hard work they were doing all the time. He imagined them going home dead tired at the end of the day, physically exhausted. He wondered if he could get a job like that, maybe something simpler, but still in the same vein. Maybe a gas station job like in an old-fashioned gas station of which there were still a couple in Waveland, so that instead of sitting in Greta's house looking out the windows at the trees, the fallen leaves blowing around, the bright light, the browning grass, the dull gray of the fence, the empty lots, and now-exposed and cleaned-up slabs the other houses had rested on, he could be at a gas station making himself useful. He'd sit around and wipe his hands on those red rags, or those blue rags that some places use, and he'd have a couple of full-service pumps, so he'd have plenty of people to talk to, and he might meet some new persons of interest, say stuff like "How're you doing?" and "Where're you headed?" and "What about this weather?" and "It's a good-looking car you've got here. What year is that?" He could do that all afternoon. He could do it for minimum wage. That wouldn't be too bad. Buy some food, some cigarettes, some alcohol. He could have a uniform—there was something wonderful about a uniform. He hadn't had a uniform since Boy Scouts. He hadn't liked the Cub Scout uniform, but the Boy Scout one was fine. He wore a uniform when he went to Catholic grade school—khakis and khaki shirt. All of the kids the same. He liked that. He missed that now. If he had a uniform it would have his name on it, or some funny name he'd make up—"Spider" or something like that on a patch over the left breast pocket, with the quotes around it. He'd have a tire gauge and a pen in his pocket, maybe a pad to write things on. He'd keep his uniforms pretty clean, but not too clean—fresh washed, but not pressed. Or maybe he'd have them done at the laundry so that they'd be stiff with starch. He thought that was the kind of thing he'd have to figure out once he got into the thing. Try one way then try another to see which he preferred. He'd have to choose his gas station carefully. He wouldn't want to be in just any gas station. Some old-fashioned gas stations are unattractive. Not much of a job for a man of his age. Certainly he could do better. He had done better, but he was never doing exactly what he wanted to do. Now and again a person should do what he wanted to.

He had worked at a gas station when he was a kid, just a few weeks one summer. He also worked in grocery stores, in a laundry, in a drugstore; he remembered all those, but didn't remember the gas station all that well. He didn't have a paper route either, though he helped this guy named Bubba with his paper route sometimes. He liked to roll the papers, holding that string in his mouth, whipping it around the paper after he'd rolled it, snapping the string when done. Sometimes on Saturdays, when the paper was really thin, they folded the pages into little, tucked-in squares, skidded them onto the driveways like stones on a lake.

The idea of staying at his old house with Gail was uncomfortable. There would be memories, emotions, awkward moments. It seemed bound to fail. But it was a big house; maybe there was enough room. Gail needed help; he cared about her, about her being in trouble, about her having a hard time. It wasn't really his job to help her get sorted out, but that didn't matter. There wasn't anyone else around to do it.

Maybe he should have insisted that he stay in the first place, instead of the divorce—retired gentleman spends his days looking out the window at leaves rattling in the breeze, sunlight sparkling in the afternoon. He rakes the yard, works the flower beds, washes the car, cleans up around the house. He could have been a house-husband. And maybe, every once in a while, he could have written his name on her neck.

After the divorce he was scared about all the terrible things that could happen to her that he would not be there to prevent. He never prevented anything terrible from happening to her in the years they were married, but when he moved out he was worried about that anyway. He kept calling her. How are you? Are you all right? Are the doors locked? Over and over, night after night.

She complained about it. She got tired of it.

What his father had complained about as he got older, into his seventies, was something that surprised Vaughn. Old people complain all the time anyway, and they are treated like duffers, as if they are buffoons and just don't understand the world they live in anymore because they are old and many changes have taken place. Others ignore their remarks and opinions, which is fine, because old people are often out of touch. But what Vaughn's father complained about was that the world had grown coarser in his lifetime. People were coarser than they had been when he was younger, Vaughn's father said. At the time Vaughn didn't think it was true, but as he grew older he began to think his father might have been right, that maybe it was inevitable that the world got dirtier and smaller and crueler with every generation. Coarser—his father's word—was the best word for it. Perhaps individuals were less supple, imaginative, compassionate—less *human*—with every generation. This was a startling proposition, to suggest that the dominant process over time was not development but deterioration.

Of course, what the world would say was that there were a lot of other explanations for this opinion of his father's, and that the opinion was ill-informed. The world would say that the world had gotten more complex and daring than it was in the past, that the world they lived in now was completely different and enormously more thrilling than ever before.

10

They moved into the house with Gail a week after she came home from the hospital. There wasn't a lot of discussion, just a quiet, uncertain drift in that direction until one night Greta suggested they do it and not worry so much. As far as Vaughn could tell, she didn't have any misgivings. She suggested he go alone, but he didn't want to do that and said so. Then they had discussions. Greta was fine with it. Gail wasn't demanding that they do it—in fact, she'd sort of apologized for asking—but it was clear to Vaughn she was still unsteady and could use the company.

"We'll be coming back here for stuff all the time anyway," Greta said. "If it goes wrong, we can just leave."

Eddie agreed to look after Greta's house. He was planning on staying in his apartment, but he brought some things inside for the sake of convenience.

At breakfast the day they were set to move Greta said, "This is not going to make any difference between us, is it?"

"No," Vaughn said. "I'd rather let it be, but I should do this for Gail."

"She still loves you," Greta said.

"I love her, too, some way or other. But that's not the deal. The deal is getting her settled down. Distracting her. Whatever."

"I know that," Greta said. "You don't have to talk me into it."

"I'm talking *me* into it," Vaughn said.

"We're doing it together," Greta said, lifting her coffee cup at him. "It's a togetherness thing. The family that saves the ex-wife together . . ."

"I don't think I'd do it without you."

"Oh, no. Of course not." Then she served the poached eggs on little pieces of toast without crusts, like rafts. The eggs looked lonely. "Can I cut them?" she said. "I like to do that."

So she cut the eggs, a single light slice across the yolk with the honed edge of the knife, like a razor cut no deeper than the skin, and the yolk oozed out over the whites, over the toast. "I am an artist of egg cutting," she said.

"Thank you," he said.

They ate silently, looking out the door at Monkey, who was on the other side of the screen looking in. "He's had his pills? Does Eddie know about the pills?" Vaughn said.

"Yes," she said. "I wrote everything down and marked the bottles."

"What about the Frontline?"

"He's got a couple weeks yet."

"Eddie can bring him over sometime," he said.

"Yeah," she said. "That'll be good."

"I'm thinking we take our stuff, make a beachhead, then head out for a movie or something. How about that?"

"No movies until one, Vaughn," Greta said.

"Just an idea," he said.

Eddie rode over to the house with them to help with the move. Vaughn thought he just wanted to be included, or maybe wanted to see where Vaughn had come from.

The house in Hidden Lake wasn't distinguished in design, or finishes, but it was more house than they'd had before—four bedrooms, three and a half baths, brick, two-story with wood floors and high ceilings, a glassed-in office off the deck, and a large kitchen. It was too big and they knew it, but they took it anyway. They got a good mortgage, so the payments weren't too bad. The lot was around an acre, maybe an acre and a quarter, and it curled along this small lake in the back and had a dead-end road in front, a cul-de-sac called Tilted Tree Lane. There were big oaks and sixty-foot pines in the front, and river birches and weeping willows out back. The house had a three-car garage, which was suddenly useful, though it had never been useful before, except as storage.

Gail had money, family money, but it didn't show up too much in the marriage. Vaughn never asked. She had people that dealt with it. She'd get mail and occasionally telephone calls, but she had little interest in the money or what she could do with it, little interest in spending it. He knew they were safe buying the house, because if worse came to worst, she could just handle it. They mentioned this, but only in passing, when they bought, and it never came up again. Her money wasn't a source of difficulty for them, though there was a sense in which they were both aware of it, a kind of lingering, out-of-sight *thing* between them.

There were four bedrooms. Under the new arrangement, Gail had the master, he and Greta took two rooms on the south side next to each other, both rooms on the front of the house looking out on the yard and the cul-de-sac. There was a balcony that ran along the outside of the house between the rooms.

Eddie came upstairs with the last of the suitcases. "This place is the shit," he said. "I'd like to live here myself."

"You've earned it," Greta said. "But you have duties in Waveland."

"There's another bedroom," Gail said, adjusting her hair as she walked into the room. "We'll make it a foursome."

Eddie did a weird little head shake. "Can't. I've got to do my research anyway. My laboratory is over there. All my paperwork is there."

"What research?" Gail said.

"He's keeping tabs on the government," Greta said.

"Yeah, just little stuff," Eddie said. "Though I'm thinking this Pentagon conspiracy deal is real."

"Which Pentagon conspiracy is that?" Gail said.

"Nine-Eleven. A lot of people think it was a rocket, maybe fired from an Air Force plane, that hit the Pentagon."

"Oh, for heaven's sake," Greta said.

"I don't make the stuff up," Eddie said. "There's a whole theory; people are all over it—lectures, photos, sound recordings, proofs of all kinds."

"Charts and graphs," Vaughn said.

"So where's the plane? Wasn't there a plane?" Gail said.

"I don't know where the plane is," Eddie said. "I think that's part of the problem."

"Where do people say the plane is?"

"They don't know where the plane is either," he said.

"It's probably still out there," Vaughn said. "Flying around. Sort of like *Mr. Arkadin.*" Everyone looked at him. He said, "Orson Welles. Very famous."

"One of Vaughn's favorites, apparently," Gail said to Greta, and they both nodded.

"I'm not a conspiracy guy," Eddie said.

"Sure you are," Greta said, dusting imaginary dust off his shoulders.

"Well, that way, maybe. It's a mean country," Eddie said.

"And yet, here you are," Gail said.

"One-handed," Vaughn said, giving her a look.

"I remember when it was a great country," Gail said. "When it was a country that did the right thing. That's what it was when we were growing up; that's what was in the history textbooks."

"I loved those books," Vaughn said.

"Quit it, will you, Vaughn?" Gail said.

"I'm trying to participate," he said.

"I'm going out," Gail said. "Will you guys be all right? It's really nice of you to move over here."

"We didn't actually *move,*" Vaughn said. "We're just coming to visit for a while."

"I know," she said. "I know exactly what's going on, and I appreciate it." She gave Vaughn a kiss on the cheek. She gave Greta a hug. She gave Eddie a handshake.

That night Vaughn and Greta had dinner in Biloxi and went to a movie. They got back late and the house was dark. Gail's car was there but her bedroom door was closed and they didn't hear anything at the door. They went out to sit on the deck and have a beer. "You think she's asleep?" Greta said.

"Could be a nap," he said. "She takes naps."

She clinked Vaughn's beer bottle with hers. "This went okay, didn't it? For the first day?"

"I guess," he said.

"Some difficulty with Eddie, there in the early going," she said.

"Where'd you get Eddie, anyway?"

"I don't know," she said. "He's been around on and off. He knows a lot of people."

"He looks like one of those weird military spooks—I mean, like I imagine those guys look."

"I get that," Greta said. "Kind of *could-explode-at-any-moment.*"

The lake was glassy and mirrored the lights in the houses across the water. They could hear the sounds of the air-conditioning units on the side of the house, the compressors working away like the industrious little angels they were.

"I wish we knew more people like him," she said. "You get people now with clever names and they don't know where to stop. They think being Pond or Able makes everything different, and suddenly they're on television or something. We should know people of good, hardworking stock. People who bowl for a living or design great buildings."

"I did not design great buildings," he said.

"Okay, maybe that was wrong," Greta said. "We should know some people who killed some people."

Vaughn gave her a squint and a raised eyebrow.

"Please," she said. "Moving along here, I'm thinking we

should know race car drivers with magic names. Or George Clooney. Or Charlie Rose. I hate him, though. He's unctuous."

"We wouldn't have to have him over," Vaughn said.

"What was your nickname when you were young?"

"Tug," Vaughn said.

"Your nickname was Tug?" she said.

"I just said that to be interesting."

"You're making fun of me," she said.

She took a long drink from her beer, and he took a long drink from his, and they sat quietly listening to the sounds of the night. They could hear cars and crickets, electronics, water, ducks. The balcony had a white rail made of wood. It seemed kind of springy with his feet on it. Across the lake, a matter of four hundred yards, other houses were barely lit up. Sometimes they could make out someone crossing a window or opening a door, but mostly it was just small yellow squares in the inky darkness of trees against a night sky.

He was worried about what was to come. Was it a good idea to stay at the house? Would it help Gail? He thought he knew what she felt like. You get to a point and things that used to mean something don't mean what they used to mean. The game changes. You don't want what you used to want. You don't care about what you used to care about. You don't need what you used to need. The whole world becomes a backdrop, a kind of cartoonish painting at the rear of the stage to which you pay not much attention. You only half listen to what people say, you only half see what's out the window. Sometimes you see people in stores or restaurants and you can't understand how they got there, what they think they're doing, why they're got-up so, why they're trying so hard, what they're after, what they hope for, what they wish. It's impossible to figure these things out and you don't care anyway. You drift through the days. They come and go.

It's funny. You can still go through the motions; you can still do what you've always done—go to work, go to dinner, talk to people—but it rolls off you. If you're lucky you take up with somebody like Greta. She's charming and funny, and you're happy to have a companion whose view of things is not altogether different from your own. You live in her garage apartment for a couple of months, and you imagine things happening, and you manage to make friends with her to a sufficient degree so that you are invited to move into the house. You take up this new position with enthusiasm, but even that is a little manufactured. You don't know what she thinks or what she is planning or what she is looking for or why she's invited you in; but you go, nonetheless, and accept the room that is offered and arrange its parts elegantly, simply. You try not to detract. You try to listen, but sometimes you just slide away in your mind.

Sometimes, when you are putting your arms around this new woman it seems as if you are remembering your role, your lines, as if your *ability* to put your arms around someone is somehow reduced. Sometimes, when you touch the skin of her face, it only reminds you of having touched the cheek of a person you were once crazy about. You smell her hair. You shut your eyes, smelling her hair. You hold her close, her back to you, smelling her hair. Your eyes closed, your hands on her forearms, on the backs of her hands. You feel her weight against you, and you remember when you felt the weight of someone you were desperate about. In short, you mimic yourself, and you wonder, Does she know? It doesn't destroy your connection to her, which is quiet, genuine, caring. Comforting, but lacking, perhaps, in intensity. The wind doesn't mean everything the way it did once. The rain is not shot through with the richest melancholy; it is just rain. This is a substantial loss.

Greta got up, scraping her chair against the deck. "I need another beer. What about you?"

"Sure," he said. "You want me to get it?"

"I'll go," she said. "I need to repair myself. Back in a flash." She went inside, leaving him on the deck. He got up and stretched and leaned against the rail, leaned out to look around the eave of the house at the moon, which was egg-shaped and glowing in the sky. "She wants friends with interesting names. But not *too* interesting," he said to no one, to the lake. "She ought to have friends first." He sat down again and propped his bare feet on the white railing, silhouetted against the dark water. He regarded the length of his first and second toes as similar. Bad for dancing. Ducks flew by and splashed into the water, quacking. He rocked and waited for Greta.

When she returned, she had beer and peanuts, a jacket, and a grin on her face. "You know, I think we ought to get things straight, like what we're doing together," she said.

"Oh, let's don't," he said. "I want an interesting name. Blackie, maybe. How about that? Call me Blackie. I'll be interesting in an angry way. I'll be angry about everything—TV, people, the government, my too-successful brother. I'll be angry about me and you."

"You're already most of that," Greta said. "Why about us?"

"We're not thirty."

"Right," she said, pretending to take a note. "Wants a thirty-year-old."

"If she could be on a leash," Vaughn said. "So I could stop her from saying things I don't want to hear and doing things I don't want done and from putting on improper clothing."

"*The Disciplinarian,*" Greta said.

"Thirty may be a little old," he said.

"Wow!" she said. "The eighty-four-mile-per-hour fastball."

"Nasty. You're nasty for an old girl," he said.

"I am not nasty. That's for sure. I'm here by the lake with you and your ex. Living life to the fullest."

"We're bound to be dead any minute," he said. "Figuratively speaking we're dead already."

"We are not. We watch *Oprah.* We watch HGTV. We cling to the reality show of the moment. *Design Star.* We're right here. We're physically here, three-dimensionally here. We don't *look* dead."

"We're debris," he said.

"Oh, please," she said. "We're as good as anybody—Gail, Eddie, the kids in their cars screwing. Are they debris? People in the movie theaters, or the people making the movies? Same, same. Being debris is some idea you have. Probably came from your dead father—"

There was a bit of silence then. He listened to her crunch her peanuts. A V-shaped ripple crossed the surface of the lake as a duck, which he couldn't actually see, swam away from them toward a light on the far shore.

"Sorry," Greta said. "I didn't mean to mention your father. Are you going to start?"

"Pardon me?" he said.

"On your father. Are you going to start?"

"No, I am not going to start," he said.

"Where are the roaches? Shouldn't there be roaches out here? I guess winter's coming. Besides, she probably has the place sprayed every fifteen minutes," Greta said. "I know that sounds hostile, but I didn't mean to be hostile. I think that's a good thing. If I could afford it, I'd get sprayed every fifteen minutes. I mean, my house."

"Gotcha," he said.

"I think we should go out to a casino and gamble," Greta said. "Right now."

"What time is it?"

"I think it's one, maybe two," she said.

"Too much trouble," he said. "You get excited and think you're a dangerous creature on dangerous ground. You throw away more money to be more dangerous, more thrilling. You swagger and wear cowboy boots, which make you taller and make you swagger, a double bonus. But then you remember the adage: *Be not the cowboy who owns no horse.*"

"You have boots in your closet. I saw them," Greta said.

"My father was very matter-of-fact when he died," he said.

"Here we go," she said.

"No, I just remember how matter-of-fact he could be. And he could be matter-of-fact at the most inopportune times," he said. "Everyone thought it was insensitivity."

"Was it?" Greta said.

"I don't know," he said. "When Gail's mother called to tell her that her father died, I answered the phone. Her mother told me what had happened, and I went in the other room and woke Gail and said to her, 'Your mother's on the phone. Your father died,' and I handed her the phone."

"Oh, man," Greta said. "That's harsh."

"I just remembered it," he said. "I don't know why I did that."

"It didn't occur to you to let the mother tell her?"

They both heard the garage door open, so they looked back across the yard in that direction. They could see in through the kitchen window, and out through the kitchen door, as the garage door rolled up and Gail's car backed right out into the street and shot away.

Vaughn turned to Greta and said, "What's that?"

"Looks like your wife is going out."

"Where's she going? It's two in the morning. You just said."

"It's past two," Greta said. "It was two a while ago. I don't know. Maybe she's going to get a sandwich? Take a drive?"

"Fuck," he said. "Come on, let's go."

"We're following her?"

They went inside, upstairs to their rooms for shoes and such, then back downstairs and out the back door and into Greta's car.

There wasn't a lot of activity on the streets of Pass Christian at that time in the morning. They'd been too slow leaving the house, so they couldn't find Gail. They went straight out to the beach highway and looked at each other, trying to figure out which way to go.

First they went west to the bay bridge. Nothing there.

"She can't be here," Vaughn said, pointing at the closed bridge. There were few cars out. For a while they didn't see anybody, then they came up behind a pickup in Henderson Point going east and a cop going at high speed but without the siren. They followed the beach highway heading east. The night was chilly, and they let the windows in the car down. They drove past a pyramidical church that had survived the storm. It had lit-up steeples, veils of spotlights shooting off into the sky above it.

"Catholic," Greta said. "Strange, huh?"

They drove through Pass Christian, Long Beach, Gulfport, and over to Biloxi. The coast was eerily empty. The year-long leftover mess from Katrina lining the highway was shocking in the moonlight. When they got to the Beau Rivage Greta said, "You want to go in?"

The casino wasn't as gaudy as the old casinos. It didn't look like a thirty-story pinball machine.

"You might have a good time," she said.

"I don't have money," he said.

"I have money," she said. She turned into the parking garage and they swirled up the ramps until she tucked the car into a parking space between two white SUVs. "Let's do a walk-through."

"And give up on Gail?" he said.

"We're not going to find Gail out there tonight," Greta said. "If she left, she had someplace to go. Let her go."

Inside, the Beau Rivage was all casino cliché—intricate purple carpet, nonstop dinging, too many people, row on row of blinking slots, a gold ceiling, piped-in rock hits blanketing everything, guys in white shirts and string ties, women in tiny skirts and push-up bras, a surplus of chatter. They stopped at the dice table.

"You played blackjack, right?" Greta said. "You played the tables in there?" She pointed to the high-stakes pavilion.

"Yes, I did. Night after night. Now, let's go somewhere else."

"Are you afraid?" she said. "We're just walking through, looking at it."

"I don't want to look at it. I'd rather be outside somewhere looking at I don't know what—beavers at the lake. Nutria."

"You've got nutria in that lake?" Greta said.

"One. We took a picture of it. Tried to tell the people in the neighborhood it was a nutria and that we should leave it alone, but they killed it. They had guns."

"Do you know the true history of the nutria?" she said.

"I don't," he said.

"This guy brought them up from South America and was going to farm them, do something with them, sell them for food or something. Brought them to Louisiana, but they multiplied like rabbits, and then there was a hurricane or something that blew them off his nutria farm, and now they are a plague upon this nation."

"Ours looked like a beaver," he said. "With a rat's tail."

"Rat beaver," she said.

One of the fifty-dollar blackjack tables was operational—one guy playing, one watching. Two other tables had dealers but no customers. There was a short guy in a suit, the pit boss. Greta nudged Vaughn and sat down at an empty table. The dealer, a woman in her twenties with curly gold hair, started to shuffle. She had six decks it looked like, a shoe to deal from. The shuffle was elaborate. It involved shuffling various sections of the six decks of cards and placing them on the felt table, then combining the piles in specific ways. Eventually she got the six decks together, Greta cut with the yellow card, and the dealer put the cards into the shoe. Greta pulled out a credit card.

"This is a fifty-dollar table," the dealer said. "If you want to play smaller stakes tables they're out there." She pointed to the main floor of the casino.

"We know," Greta said. She dropped the card on the table.

Without looking away, the dealer moved the credit card to her right and called the pit boss.

Greta asked for five hundred dollars' worth of chips. "Sit," she said to Vaughn.

"We ought to go out there," he said, pointing to the cheaper tables.

"I want to play here," she said. "It's more fun here."

"Does any of this look like fun?" he said, waving at the room.

"Not yet," she said. "Just hang on. I didn't tell you, but I'm a blackjack genius."

She got twenty chips, all green. She put two on the circle in front of her, and waited for cards. First hand out she got sixteen against a face card for the dealer. Greta hit, got a four, stood, and won fifty dollars. Second hand she got a blackjack. Third hand she got a pair of aces, which she split and got two face cards. Fourth hand she got a three and a seven and an ace when she hit. It went on like that for a while. When she was twelve hundred dollars up, she waved a hand at the dealer to stop. "Color me up, will you?" she said. The dealer did, and they walked over to the cage to pick up the money.

"Nicely done," Vaughn said.

"Happens all the time," she said. "Whenever I play. If you only play a few hands, you come out ahead."

"Is that a mathematical certainty?"

"It's magic," she said. "I saw it on TV. Blackjack is like flipping a coin. If flips start going your way, keep flipping."

"So if you lose the first few hands?"

"Quit," she said. "Try again later."

She was hungry, so they went upstairs where there was a little café. He had pancakes. They were good—puffy and covered with whipped cream and strawberries and drizzled with maple syrup. Sick but good. Greta ate off his plate.

"We shouldn't be doing this, you know," he said. "My heart."

"It'll be fine. We'll work out tomorrow in that gym back at the castle."

"No gym, sorry," he said.

"I can't believe you actually bought that house," Greta said. "I mean, it's a really big, really ugly, brick house."

"I don't think it's that ugly," he said.

"I don't mean it's *ugly,* but it's that kind of house—it's a banker's house."

"If only," he said.

11

When they got home, Gail's car was locked up tight in the big garage and no light was escaping under the master bedroom door, so there wasn't much left for Vaughn and Greta to do. They sat in Vaughn's room for a bit.

"How long are we doing this?" she asked.

"Got no idea," he said. "Maybe just a week or two, maybe longer. You think it's crazy?"

"Yeah, it's a little crazy, but I don't mind. It's a change of pace. And I like seeing your house. She didn't change much, did she? It was like this when you were here?"

"Uh-huh," he said. "Seems funereal now. More drapey."

"It has this 'you have arrived at your destination' feel to it," Greta said. "Reminds me of the house I had with Bo. It's not a good feeling."

"It's a bird around your neck. Like, how will you ever get away?"

"Your husband gets killed," Greta said.

"We should talk," he said.

"I shouldn't say that," Greta said.

"You're among friends."

"I am, aren't I?" she said, gripping his shoulder in a surprisingly stout way. "Still, it's not something to take lightly, not a good idea to treat things that way."

"Maybe it's healthy," Vaughn said.

"Okay. We can drive around and I can point out the sites where my husband beat me. 'Here's where he came after me with a belt when I burned the steak,' " she said, mockpointing.

"Ah, the memories," Vaughn said.

"The good news is that in the end he took one for the team."

"Greta—"

"Sorry."

She stayed with Vaughn for a while longer, then said she was tired and wanted to sleep, so kissed him most circumspectly and went off to her room.

Vaughn didn't feel much like sleep. He wandered down to the kitchen thinking that he really wanted to go back to Greta's house and watch television until daylight, then sleep until the afternoon. It was too spooky being back in his house. It had been dumb to come. Surely his being there was worse for her, especially if she was still having trouble going on. He thought it might keep Tony away, but with Gail going off in the middle of the night, that wasn't working. Gail was always a bit erratic, a little scary, prone to act quickly, as if hit with a cattle prod. It had been hard to figure her out when they were married, and it was harder now. Sometimes she seemed brilliant, gifted; sometimes she just seemed nuts. The stunt with Tony was typical, right up to where he beat her up—that was new. Still, a hopelessly wrong guy was par for the course. She'd done that before when they had trouble. There was the sign painter, a big heavyset guy with arms like Popeye; he turned out about the opposite of the way he looked. There was an alcoholic who wasn't allowed to drive but owned a big black truck in which he and Gail sped up and down the beach highway for a while, her at the wheel. One summer she even brought home a guy she met at the beach in Florida, a shave-his-head type with a cocky grin and artificial manners.

Vaughn had been no saint. The worst was a woman at the office in Dallas. He and Gail were doing a trial separation. So he was with this other woman all the time. She was attractive, a designer at the firm. They spent nights together. They spent weeks together. They had sex. They went to dinner. They went to movies, to the zoo, for drives into rainy nights, to old restaurants with big wooden booths and white tablecloths. It looked like romance, but the truth was that Vaughn couldn't make himself care for the woman. She smelled odd. She didn't look right in the bed. She didn't act right. She didn't say the right things. She had a hard, brittle voice. He missed Gail. At the worst times he wept, and the woman held him. Try to imagine that now.

They talked. She told him about her father, how her mother had abandoned her to her father. An ugly story, complete with details about her father slipping into the bathroom when she was a teenager coming home from a date, slipping his furry fingers into the waistband of her panties. The woman only wanted a decent relationship, and Vaughn gave her none of that. Eventually he and Gail patched things up.

Years later he ran into the woman at a conference in Chicago. She was married and hoping to start a family. She and Vaughn had some drinks and a desultory tryst, sex in the hotel, all the usual; and in the aftermath some friend of her husband's saw them walking out of the hotel. He threatened to blow the whistle, so she ended up going to dinner with him. Vaughn left the conference early, never found out what happened.

He tried calling her a few weeks later, tried a couple of times, but she was done with him. The calls were short and deadly.

He thought now that they were probably too easygoing about such things in their marriage. The affairs were expected, assumed, allocated even, probably as much a matter of protection as anything—the air bags of their marriage. If you knew a wreck was coming, it didn't hurt to plan ahead. On the other hand, maybe the planning made the wrecks a little more likely, a little more frequent.

Vaughn was rinsing a knife after making himself a peanut butter sandwich on raisin bread. The bread was older than it should have been. The knife had made a piercing metallic sound drawn against the other knives when he pulled it from the drawer. It was part of the silverware set she'd ordered from the Museum of Modern Art. Very handsome, now very old. He folded the sandwich up inside a doubled Bounty paper towel, caught the light switch with the sandwich as he left the kitchen. He walked through the dark house looking at the stuff he'd once owned with Gail—the furniture, the pictures, the knickknacks on the shelves. Nothing much had moved in the year since he left, and yet he felt as though he was in one of his neighbors' houses—somebody he did not know well or want to know well, just another person of about the same age, the same financial condition, the same limited vision. He shook his head at the stuff. The furniture was nondescript, the lamps were knockoffs of better lamps they couldn't afford or thought foolishly expensive. The couch—why had he even bought a couch? Useful, maybe, but impossibly ugly, certainly. Where had the training gone, the belief, the desire to furnish the house well, to buy only beautiful things? When had the fatigue set in, and comfort and ease become more important than quality and provenance?

He knew that *everybody* had crap in their houses, that all the houses he'd endlessly studied for so many years in *Architectural Record, Domus,* and dozens of other magazines that were the backbone of his real architectural study, were just fantasies, set pieces, tableaux, even if the world they suggested was one he had spent much of his life longing for the way a kid longs for the treats of Christmas morning.

Vaughn went upstairs eating his sandwich. He couldn't remember what it felt like to be desperately in love. He felt almost nothing for Gail by now, though he knew his role and duty, and accepted those without question. He was comfortable seeing to her when she needed a hand. With Greta there was something more, something about prospects, just the suggestion of possibility—a small, certain warmth; less responsibility, more ease.

He sat on his bed and tried to remember feelings he'd had but drew a blank. He could remember being in love with Gail many years before, but like so many things, the memory was by now just the name of the thing.

You don't plan to lose that stuff, those feelings, but you become a different person over time, with different borders and parameters, different ideas, different ways of functioning. What you used to do you don't do anymore. You can't. You won't. So maybe the wife or girlfriend gets something short of your full romantic capacity. And you do, too. Pretty soon romance is diagrammatic.

He was thinking about that word *diagrammatic* when there came a little tick on his bedroom door, and then the knob turned and the door opened and Gail was standing silhouetted against the hall light.

"Can I come in?" she said.

"Sure," he said.

The only light in the bedroom was coming from the hall. Gail picked her way across the room, sat on the edge of the bed.

"Where did you go when you went out?" he said.

"I just went out for a while," she said. "I had some things to do. I had to think."

"What about?"

"What do you think I was thinking about?" she said.

"Puppies?" he said. Even though he couldn't see her shaking her head, he could see her shaking her head. "Sorry," he said.

"I was thinking about you and me, and your girlfriend," she said. "And Tony. And about what happened."

"With Tony?" he said. "Or with us?"

"Both," she said. "Tony and everything else. I was thinking about me and this house. I went out for a drive. Sometimes I like to get out."

"In the middle of the night," he said.

"Yes," she said. "In the middle of the night. It's quiet. It's dark. There aren't so many people. You can drive around un-encumbered. I smoke in the car."

"I don't think you ought to smoke," he said.

"I don't in the house. You never let me smoke in the house, and I don't like to smoke much anyway, but in the car I like to smoke. I like the sound of the engine, the feel of the air conditioner, the smell of the smoke, the smell of my breath as I draw it in and blow it out."

"All of that?" he said.

"I want you to stay with me," she said.

"I'm here. We're here. We've come to stay for a while," he said.

"No, I mean I want *you* to stay."

"Permanently?" he said.

"Yes," she said.

"I don't see how I can do that," he said. "Not now."

"It's only been a year," she said.

"A year is a long time," he said.

"Just give it a try," she said. She reached out and touched his hand and started playing with it the way she always played with his hand. "Greta can stay, too," she said. "Maybe. Maybe all three of us can live here. We'll just be friends. That's mostly what we were, right?"

"Well, more than that. We were friends, lovers, partners. Husband and wife," he said.

"But it really came down to friends. After all the fucking was done."

"That's not quite true," he said. "Not even after the fucking. There was something else—some tenderness."

"There was a lot of tenderness," she said.

"Right. That's what I mean."

"So where's that now?" she said.

"You got a cigarette?" he said.

"Not in the house," she said. "Where's that tenderness now?"

"I don't know," he said. "Gone away. Too old for tenderness."

"Pish," she said.

"Why does everybody say that?" he said. "Pish. Everybody I know says pish now."

"You don't know so many people, do you?" she said.

"Guess not," he said.

She crooked a finger at him and led him out of the bedroom, down the hall, into their old bedroom. It looked different, both better and worse. Looked like it was right out of West Elm or something—lots of semi-designer furniture carefully placed, good-looking fabrics, lots of earth colors. It was, above all, tasteful, even sort of serene. He was surprised how much he liked the way she'd fixed it up. In the whole house it was the only room she'd changed.

"I do, actually, have cigarettes," she said, opening a drawer in one of the nightstands.

"Came to my senses," he said, standing by the French doors. He pulled back the drapes on either side. The light was just coming into the sky outside. Off to the right, where the lake made a dogleg, the water was all mirrored up. He could hear the birds waking up or whatever it is they do that makes them chirp and cry in the mornings. There was a sliver of white moon way off to the west.

"This is nice," he said. "You're nice, Gail."

She crossed the room and stood beside him at the window, and they looked out at the lake and the pier, painted white, and the church beyond the houses on the other side of the lake, with its white steeple pointing up into the thinly lit sky. She pushed open the French doors out onto the balcony, and they stood there in the doorway for a few minutes. She hooked her arm in his, rested her head on his shoulder. Ducks were silhouetted against the reflected lake light.

"I don't need so much," she said.

"A good thing," he said. "I don't have much."

"Don't be mean," she said.

"I'm not being mean," he said. "I'm just, like, honest. You kind of caught me at a bad time here."

"Tonight?" she said.

"Rest of my life."

"Good to know," she said. She intertwined her fingers with his and wrapped her left hand around his arm, leaned harder. "It could be a lot worse."

"I'm supposed to be telling you that," he said.

"Yeah, I know," she said. "I'm just helping you out." She stepped out on the balcony and lit up a cigarette. He followed her.

The balcony faced north and they were close to the lake, so they had horizon all the way east to west. There were chairs. The chairs were wet. Neither of them mentioned it. They sat together without saying anything for a while. The light in the east came up as if on the world's biggest rheostat. It was something to see. Dusky blue at the horizon turning rose, then orange, then pink, then a little green before the whole lighter blue of the sky running up forty-five degrees and turning darker again. Stars still sat up there in the darkness. Vaughn and Gail could just make out each other, hands and feet, the railing, the chairs. They stared out over the water. There were trees all around the lake so their horizon was black silhouettes against the less dark sky. Occasionally a bird shot over the house. Vaughn heard wings beating the air. Gail tapped his arm and pointed to the lawn on the other side of the garage, in the strip of land that ran down to the pier, where six ducks, dark against the brown of the grass, hustled around pecking for food, straightening their feathers.

"They were just kids a couple weeks ago," Gail said. "The four on the left. Now look at them."

Above the pier the pink from the lowest tier of light had come down to rest at the other edge of the lake so that the treetops were now reflected along the shore, and above them, in the water, the pink sky, the lighter blue. A heron swung by out of nowhere, cutting diagonally across in front of them and sailing to a spot on the far side of the lake.

"It's not so bad, is it?" Gail said.

"It's *Rome Adventure,*" he said.

"The movie or the book?"

"I don't think there was a book."

"Oh, my god," she said. "Forgive me."

"You're forgiven, but let's don't mention it again," he said.

"Christian Bale and Madonna," she said. "I don't know."

"Keep going," he said. "You'll get there."

"Dakota Fanning," she said, pointing the glowing ash of her cigarette at him.

"Now you're cooking," he said.

"You've still got that *young* thing," she said.

"Not really. Not too young."

"A guy at the office who's sixty-five has a two-year-old daughter."

"And the wife?" he said.

"Late thirties," she said. "He's very excited about it, too. Everybody seems to be excited for him. I personally think it's disgusting, of course."

"He sired this child when he was beyond sixty?" Vaughn said.

"I believe that's correct," she said.

"Oh holy night," he said.

"Well, I just thought you ought to know," Gail said. "I thought you ought to keep that in mind. Anything's possible. The world is still open to you." She paused for a minute and patted his arm.

He looked at her, trying to figure out what she was thinking.

"Nah," she said. "Just kidding."

"Gee, thanks," he said.

"Look at this white light over here," she said.

He looked. She was right. It *was* something. Above the trees in the east the sky had gone sweet and creamy. Aerosol whipped-topping white.

12

Ten days sailed by with minimum incident. Gail was missing in action a couple of nights, one overnight, but there were no visible wounds; and so, during this period, the three of them were a happy, if elaborated, family. They sat on the deck and watched ducks in the evenings. The third or fourth time they convened on the deck there were dozens of ducks about, maybe two dozen, squawking and running after one another in the grass at lake's edge. There were five swans—two full grown, white, and three that were younger, leggy and still gray. It was late afternoon.

"Are these swans doing the right thing?" Greta asked. "Is this the right time of year for them to have these babies?"

"They're late," Gail said. "Maybe a month, maybe two, seems like."

Vaughn had in mind the duck scene from the first season of *The Sopranos*. Tony by the pool, dreaming of another life.

He had no idea about Greta. He never knew what she was thinking anyway. She was probably thinking about poisoning him the way women poisoned men on Court TV. Or maybe she was thinking about swans—how they're made, why they have those feet, what are feathers? It would be like Greta to look it up in the wildlife book her husband had given her.

Vaughn said, "You have that bird book. You could look it up."

"What, Bo's bird book? How do you know about that?"

"Saw it at your house," he said. "One day. You weren't there. It's inscribed."

"I know that," Greta said. "What, do I look like I'm pining away for Bo here? Not on your life. I'm Lucky Girl."

"Annie Oakley," Gail said. Then she looked up, caught the expression on Greta's face. "Just kidding," Gail said. "Joking around."

"Don't you start, too," Greta said.

"Too?"

"Yeah. Your husband has the morbid curiosity blues every once in a while."

"He's not my husband," Gail said.

"Right. Sometimes I forget, you know?" She turned back to Vaughn. "I just don't picture you creeping around the house going through my things."

"Ease up, will you? I pulled a book out of a bookcase."

Greta waggled her hand. "You're right. Sorry. Just caught me by surprise. And I am lucky, after what happened to Gisele—her face, all that. I could be Girl With One Eye, but instead here I am with you, watching these ducks."

Gail said, "They come because of the lake. If we didn't have the lake we wouldn't have the ducks."

"That's right, honey," Greta said.

"So he did that to her on purpose?" Vaughn said. "Ran her into that building or whatever it was?"

"It was a garage," Greta said. "And, yes. He was a bastard."

This was typical Greta-talk. Passing reference to the trouble she'd seen. Sometimes it was drug-related, her life on the lam in Los Angeles years before, skittering across town in the middle of the night in skimpy garments after being tossed out of a moving car by her husband, Bo, who was at that time a lowlife hanger-on in the screenwriting business. Her story was that he'd written one pathetic screenplay for some one-shot director and it had gone exactly nowhere, and this produced in Bo the realization that his life was unfair. From this he took his charter to heap manure on others near and dear, and that meant Greta mostly, and mostly Greta did not talk about it. Gisele was one of Bo's priors.

Later, of course, Bo took the big sleep.

Vaughn wasn't sure Gail knew what they were talking about, and he was going to say something by way of explanation, when Greta gave him a little cockeyed wave of the head that he figured meant leave it alone. So he turned back to the ducks.

The ducks were quacking a lot more than was attractive. They were also shitting on the lawn, or doing something that looked like shitting. He was thinking they probably weren't shitting, that they probably did that in the water, when they were sitting there, floating along, paddling, or whatever they did. He was thinking they must be doing something else on the lawn, but the way they wagged their butts it looked like shitting.

"What are they doing out there?" he said. "You see this?" He pointed at a duck with one of those iridescent green bands around its neck. "The mallard, there, or whatever it is. That a mallard? Whatever—you see what it did?"

"It's walking," Greta said. "They walk funny. You'd walk funny if your feet were spatulas."

Gail got up and leaned on the railing. "It feels like when I used to be grounded."

"You are kind of grounded," he said.

"Ah, man," she said. "That's crap."

"We need you," Greta said. "Without you we'd get on each other's nerves so bad. I mean, there's trouble here."

"You should go on a retreat," Vaughn said. "Take a couple of weeks in the convent with the Sisters of Mercy. You'd be in there with the big drapes and the smelly furniture. Who knows? Maybe you'd like it?"

"I *would* like it," Greta said. "That's been proven."

"I'd go, too," Gail said. "I'd be like some sainted nun."

"You wouldn't be able to sneak out for meetings with Cheech," Vaughn said.

"Don't call him that," Gail said. Then she stopped a minute, as if an idea had come to her. "Maybe I should go to church, like tonight. Anybody for church?"

Vaughn got up and put an arm around her shoulder. She was steady, no shrugging him off. "I could go to church," he said. "We could move in there. Think they'd mind?"

"Don't discourage her if she wants to go to church," Greta said. "He wants to go all the time," she said to Gail. "Talks about it, anyway."

Vaughn threw bread to the ducks. They quacked like crazy. The sun was missing in action, cloud-obscured, making the afternoon pleasant, almost winterlike. He hugged Gail and kissed her temple, and, as he pulled back, caught a glimpse down her shirt of her small breasts in a padded bra. He looked away quick, tossed more bread, and more bread, a fever of bread tossing.

"Eat up, guys," he said to the ducks. "Life is short."

"Is not," Gail said, pulling the loaf out of his hand. She fished out a slice and started chewing on it.

"Don't these ducks belong to somebody?" he said.

Gail sighed and shook her head. "Wild," she said. "They're wild ducks."

"They saw the water and landed, right?" Greta said.

"Mrs. Posey got the swans," Vaughn said. "So why is it strange to think maybe she got the ducks, too?"

"Mrs. Posey is the head of the Swan Committee," Gail said. "The swans were eight hundred apiece. That's what she said. And when they have babies we have to give the babies back to the people who sold us the swans. That's the deal. She said she would have paid for the swans herself if the board hadn't approved."

"If I had an air rifle I could use these ducks for target practice," Vaughn said.

Air rifle. It had been a while. Probably the ducks would have waddled away at high speed with the sound of the first shot. Not to mention the projectile itself. These ducks were particularly pretty, he thought, in an iridescent way. And he didn't want to shoot them, though he had shot at turtles from their neighbor Bill Ansen's deck one night several summers before. He used to see Bill Ansen out there all the time shooting into the water, but who knew he was shooting turtles? Then Vaughn went over there one evening and Bill Ansen showed him how much fun it was, shooting at the turtles swimming in the lake. The pellets just ricocheted off the turtles' backs, Bill Ansen said. He was a great guy, Bill Ansen. But then he died.

"I think I will go to church," Gail said.

"Me, too," Greta said.

"You're going to church, too?" Vaughn said.

"Sure. Won't hurt," Greta said. "People go to church all the time. So, yeah, we're going to church. Right, Gail? We're going to kneel in the pews. We're going to say some prayers, and ask forgiveness, and like that. We may stay there all night long. We may never leave."

"I think I'm going, too," he said.

"I like the way church smells," Gail said. "That's the main thing."

"That *is* the main thing," Vaughn said, flipping the remaining four slices of bread into the air, one after the other, in the direction of the ducks. The slices spun like edible Frisbees and seemed to linger, weightless, in the air, before falling to earth.

13

Eddie came over for Thanksgiving dinner and stayed to watch *World Series of Poker* reruns, and he got so pissed Vaughn thought he was going to wreck the place. Vaughn had to change the channel to calm Eddie down. He switched to the Discovery Channel and after a few minutes of some travel program Eddie started attacking the hosts of that program.

"You suck," he said. "You bunch of fucks. I mean, who'd have thought you could get paid to go around and look at old towns and shit? I mean, I could fucking do that. I've been some places."

Gail said she was tired and was going to get into her pj's, and left the three of them in the TV room. Eddie hated everything, which made him a perfect companion for Vaughn; but Vaughn didn't want Eddie to know that, or maybe he didn't want to admit that they had the same view of people on television. Eddie divided the world into the people on television and the rest of humanity, and in this division the people on television came out on the short end of things.

Vaughn kept cycling through the channels. He caught a lot of football, and some other holiday fare. He tried to pacify Eddie with a late NFL game, but no luck. He tried a stop on the agricultural channel, but Eddie had some choice things to say about the cows. Then they hit some news channels.

"Fucking Arabs," Eddie said. "They're fucking everywhere. I'm over at the house watching the big screen and I just can't get away from them. What're these guys here doing?"

He gestured toward the screen where there were some street scenes in some town somewhere—maybe Iraq, maybe Afghanistan. Guys in robes, some huts, the usual. A few big cars coming through in a motorcade of some sort.

"What're they doing?" Eddie said. "They should wash up or something. They should get running water, for fuck's sake."

"Easier said than done," Greta said. "It's like a desert over there."

"And yet, here comes somebody in a fucking Mercedes-Benz!" Eddie said. He pointed at the TV. "These people really burn me up. This is like some bad television show that some producer sold the studios and now we have to fucking watch it for ten years." He got up and shook his head, glaring at the TV. He slapped his forehead with his palm and pointed at the screen with his stump. "Jesus Christ, Jesus Christ, Jesus Christ," he said, quoting somebody.

Greta motioned for Vaughn to change the channel, so he flipped through a few and got to one of the HD channels where they were running an old episode of *Sunrise Earth*—a lovely marsh with some mountains in the distance, a speck-led white horse in the foreground up to its ankles in water, drinking, then swishing its head around, tossing water drops every which way.

"Now you're talking," Greta said.

"It's god-awful sandy over there," Eddie said. "I don't blame those people. I knew a bunch of them. They were fine. Maybe a little bit excitable, but they were fine. Thing is, you look at them and pretty quick you figure out what's going on. I mean, you thought Catholics were bad? They are nothing compared to these people. These people are fucking terrified that God is going to rip out their eyes, split their tongues, drive nails through other parts. They're screwing the sheep and God knows what else, but they are *so* terrified. They pray hard over there. Hard, I'm talking. That's when I really understood them, when I saw that. They are God-fearing fuckers, what God might do, what trouble he might visit on them. He'll make the goat chew on the baby; that's the way he works. A giant snake will come up out of the river and steal the baby and swallow it whole, and then lay out there in the sun with this huge bulge in it where the baby is. That's the way they think. They're demented children, horrid children."

"This is a good-looking horse," Vaughn said, without turning away from the screen. "He's pretty gorgeous standing in that water, isn't he? You know anything about horses? What kind of horse is that, anyway?"

"Big and white," Greta said.

"When I was in Pasquar or Nurwat or something like that," Eddie said, "you could hardly believe it. Those people lived in a world of dirt. Incredible. Remember when they found Saddam in that hole? Multiply that a billion times and that's what the place is like. That's what those people are like. They're sweet, but the world they have is harsh. Can you imagine

124

Bush hiding in a hole somewhere? For *any* reason? I mean, his ass would hide at the drop of a hat, but, you know, in a *hotel* or something. When the fucking president of a country hides in a hole, what kind of country do you think it is to start with? I don't mean they're backward, but, Jesus, they are *some kind* of backward. What can they do? Sand in their eggs, sand in their eyes, sand in their shorts. Try putting on a rubber hat full of sand every day—"

"They wear rubber hats?" Greta said.

Vaughn clicked off the set. He turned around and looked at Eddie. Eddie looked mournful. "Sorry," he said.

"Before my father died," Vaughn said, "and it was kind of a messy death, all things considered, and I take the blame for that. I take responsibility. I loved my father but I didn't shoulder the burden when it fell to me; I didn't take care of him when he needed care, and now guilt comes and goes like a puncture wound that heals, scars, and reopens. Anyway, *before* he died, once I went over there to see him, and he was kind of short and fat, and he was having a terrible time with heat rash or something like that in his crotch; he had trouble reaching the places where the skin was abraded, and he needed help putting the medicine on, so I ended up having to put the talcum or Desenex or whatever it was on his balls because he said he couldn't see to do it himself. I told him to do it by feel, but he wouldn't, and he was a strong-willed motherfucker and he could make you do stuff just by staring you down. So there I was, him in a wheelchair with his suet-white legs spread, and me down on all fours in front of him, shaking the can and spreading this powder all over his testicles. It was like a medical snowstorm down there. It was blinding."

"Ick," Eddie said.

"I'm telling you, Eddie, you want to hire that kind of thing out. Take my word for it."

There was a silence in the room then. It was darker with the TV off. The streetlights outside sent tree limb shadows in through the windows. The room looked gargantuan, like who would have a TV room the size of a small auditorium?

"Shit," Eddie said. "That is some shit."

Greta gave Vaughn a look that he took to mean *Good work,* and then the three of them all stood up at the same time, walking toward the kitchen and the back door, where Eddie was sure to exit.

Later that Thanksgiving night Vaughn told Greta that she deserved a better companion than he could ever be, a better person, a person with fewer problems, maybe a people person.

"I dislike people people," she said. "For your information."

"I used to behave better than I do now," he said. "When you're a person of a certain age everything changes and the world"—here he swept his arms in a wide arc, the better to compass the territory to which he wanted to refer—"which used to be attractive, possibly charming at times, turns out to be a sewage hole of immense proportion, unimaginable proportion, overrun with dimwits. This knowledge doesn't encourage anybody."

"We've had a lovely holiday dinner," Greta said.

"No, we did not," Vaughn said. "We had turkey and other holiday things, but the dinner was by no means lovely. The dinner was a tragic mimicry of holiday kitsch—four empty husks repeating a performance that long ago lost meaning for all of us."

"The turkey was dry," she said.

"I don't mean the turkey," Vaughn said.

"Vaughn," she said. "I want you to listen to me. Once I fucked a guy in a gas station toilet. The men's toilet. He was a good looker, too. It had been a while. We were pumping gas at the same island in the middle of the night and we started talking, and within minutes we moved it right into the toilet. I was young and needy then, but I surprised myself with that. I had been trying to get across town. I was traveling and I'd been out a long time. The performance wasn't my finest hour, but everything still worked. Afterward we went to the local IHOP, where he seemed like a regular, and we ate a joyful dinner—greasy bacon, sloppy eggs, hotcakes on the side."

"Hmm," Vaughn said. "My kind of girl."

"I appreciate *that*," she said, giving him two hand guns.

14

A few days later Vaughn took Eddie to the Hot-2-Trot for beers. He felt guilty for running Eddie off on Thanksgiving, and said as much, apologizing.

"Happens to me all the time," Eddie said. "I don't worry about it."

They sat up on stools and watched the tattoo girl move around behind the bar. Vaughn said, "When Gail and I split I was thinking of getting some kind of dinky job, just to change things up. You know? Get out of the world I'd been in."

"Sure," Eddie said.

"You want to have some menial job that puts you on the sidelines for a while, where nothing is at stake, or at least not at stake in the way you're used to. You get up, have a clear head, nothing you're responsible for, and you go to work and sit around earning your minimum wage. And at night you go home, clean up, and then you're fresh and ready, and nothing to worry about until the next morning. It's like being a kid again."

"So did you?"

"No," Vaughn said. "I thought about working in a gas station. As you may know, I worked in a gas station for a short period when I was a kid. I don't know why that always appealed to me. Maybe the smell. But it would have to be an old gas station, not like the ones out there now."

"We still got a couple those over here," Eddie said.

"I know that, and I considered applying," Vaughn said. "But I came up short. I don't think I'm cut out for retail. Too much sneezing. People will sneeze all over you if you let them. Go to any restaurant and there's always somebody sneezing, blowing those germs out twenty-three feet or whatever it is. And that's not all of it; that's just the start, the sneezing. I don't need to tell you—"

"No," Eddie said.

"You'll walk up to a car and some guy'll let you have it just like that. No chance to escape."

Eddie seemed barely attentive. He was watching the bar girl's butt. The tattoo was much in evidence—colorful, elaborate, and it dipped in the center, like all of them do, as if to say, "Enter Here."

Vaughn said, "So I half expected Gail to bring this Tony kid over for Thanksgiving. She goes out all the time, though. Saturday she was out all night. I got worried, but Greta persuaded me to wait. I mean, I don't know where the guy lives, anyway. I don't know what we could've done."

"I heard," Eddie said. "Greta asked me to look the guy up. I'm working on the address."

Vaughn leaned away, squinted at Eddie.

"Quit it," Eddie said. "I'm just helping out. Maybe talk to him in the sweetest possible way, suggest that he, too, has something to lose."

"Don't go too far with that," Vaughn said. "Could get nasty."

Eddie tapped his bottle. "I don't mind a little nasty now and again. Keep your hand in the game, so to speak. Anyway, she asked, so that's that."

"She asked," Vaughn said.

Eddie went off to the bathroom in the back of the place, and Vaughn ordered more beer for both of them. The girl with the tattoo's name was Chandra, she said.

"What's with the tattoo?" Vaughn asked when she slid the new bottles to him, one at a time.

She reached around behind her and tugged at the waistband of her jeans. "Had it awhile," she said. "Me and some girls got them one night we were partying."

"You like tattoos?"

"They don't hurt anybody. Guys like 'em. You've been keeping an eye on it, yeah?"

"I have it under surveillance," Vaughn said, dropping money on the bar.

She smiled as she picked up the bills. "They speed things up," she said. "I don't see it very often. It's back there all the time."

Eddie got back on his stool and the girl moved away. "You hitting?" he said.

"Not now, not ever," Vaughn said.

"You know that thing you were talking about, the shit job? I did that when I got out of rehab. I got this thing at the movie theater in Gulfport. Manager. The West Gulfport Four, a fourplex where they played stuff a week or two after it left the mall."

"I always wanted a movie theater," Vaughn said.

"Doubt that," Eddie said. "I didn't do much except ride herd on the kids. They ran the place, made the eats, took tickets, started the projectors. I inherited the projection kid named Delveaux from the previous manager. Kid was pissed he didn't get the manager job, so he never started a movie on time. People would come for a three-thirty Saturday picture and at three-forty-five they'd start coming out asking where the movie was. If it got real late on a Saturday, I went upstairs to get Delveaux on the job—he'd be napping, or reading porn magazines he had stashed up there—but if it was an ordinary day, I'd just call him from the stinking hole of an office I had behind the snack counter."

"You get to pick the movies?"

"Shit," Eddie said. "You kidding? They came out of some-place in Alabama. I had nothing to do with it."

"I'm not having a theater if I can't pick the movies," Vaughn said.

"Yeah, I'll bet your movies are going to draw the big crowds," Eddie said. "They'll be waiting in the rain to get in."

"The shit. You got no idea what movies I'd show."

"*Rashômon*," Eddie said. "*Picnic.*"

"You got me," Vaughn said. "So what happened with you and these kids?"

"The kids were okay. There was the guy Delveaux, a geeky kid named Greg or something, two girls, Tink and Haley—one of them with lousy skin, both with the bodies all the kids have now. They were supposed to wear uniforms, but I let them wear whatever they wanted. That earned me some points for a while. Then the regional manager came and found them in matching tube tops."

"Cool," Vaughn said.

"Looked good to me, but the regional guy was all of eighteen and very serious. He said the outfits were unprofessional. He decided we all needed to wear white shirts. 'It'll be like a uniform,' he said. 'But it won't *feel* like a uniform.' This was his personal breakthrough, I think."

"That won't work," Vaughn said. "Cheese, nachos, butter, chocolate—even when they're clean they're filthy."

"So anyway the girls wore that bandeau stuff underneath, left the shirts open to the navel, so the regional twit didn't put me out of business."

"You're kind of skeevy in your old age, aren't you?"

"Every opportunity," Eddie said. "You take what you can get."

"You want another beer?"

"Naw," Eddie said. "I need some sleep. Anyway, the job didn't do anything for me. I didn't last long. I may have been a little *too* unprofessional with one of the girls, the one named Tink. I mean, how's a guy not fall in love with a girl named Tink? You know?"

"Amen," Vaughn said.

"Regional Man got wind of it and told me my services were no longer required. I considered ripping his face off, but then I figured that would reflect badly on me and it probably wasn't worth it in the long run. I folded tents, said good-bye to the kids, and retired from the business."

"Leaving Tink."

"Yeah, I regret that. I went back a few times, but her interest did not last. She may have been moved by mercy."

15

Saturday Gail and Greta were out shopping and Vaughn was alone at the house. He poked around in Gail's bedroom for a while, didn't find anything of interest, then draped himself across her bed. The French doors were open and the breeze was blowing across his chest and he was thinking he had less of a life than before, where "before" meant just about anything at all—twenty years ago or yesterday. It had all been a steady downward drift by his reckoning. That wasn't helping much, so he went downstairs to see what he could find in the kitchen.

He found Pepperidge Farm Orange Milano cookies, a small pleasure that he had years before introduced to his mother. She loved them. She only ate one at a sitting, but she savored it. He remembered sitting with her at the dining table while she ate a single Orange Milano after dinner with her tea. He didn't see her very often. He and Gail would visit once a year in Atlanta. When his mother was still healthy that was great. She was funny and full of oddly wised-up ideas, always presented as if she were shocking herself with her own candor. She was a woman out of an Austen book, or some other, having seen many things you would not have imagined, smart and quiet in equal measures, with miraculous timing and a gift for the language.

Vaughn took the cookies back to the TV room and turned on the set that he'd bought four or five years before, a Sony flat-screen CRT with about two hundred pounds of glass in the front. He'd researched this television for months, determined to get a set that was top of the line. Gail was appalled at the study and the price. Now Vaughn clicked it on and tuned to CNN where they were running some kind of special report on hurricanes, a seasonal wrap-up. There was footage of Anderson Cooper tying himself to giant planters in front of hotels and doing the rest of those antics he made so popular pre-Katrina. Vaughn's mother would've said "Bon voyage," or something similar. There were bright graphics about the relative strengths of various hurricanes of the last fifty years, and there were pictures of and captions about the 1900 storm in Galveston, and footage from different hurricanes in different years hitting small towns along the Gulf Coast, all of it cut together to music and hurricane sounds, with shouting reporters layered in here and there. Then there was video of people with chain saws cleaning up after. Good hurricanes make good neighbors. Lots of Katrina footage, naturally, with some stuff about the Mississippi coast he hadn't seen before.

After a while he started praying. He wasn't praying for anything in particular, just a preventive maintenance prayer, alternating remembered versions of the Hail Mary and the Our Father, sort of under his breath, sort of in his head. This wasn't the first time, or even unusual; it was something he'd started maybe ten or fifteen years ago. It just happened one day and then he started doing it on and off, like when nothing else was happening, and he was alone. In fact, he wasn't sure he would call it praying so much as reciting prayers. When he was a kid he had prayed a lot; he liked to pray all the time. He would go to the Catholic church and it was chilly inside, and thick with that sweet church scent, the light filtering in through the stained glass, big statues and flowers up by the altar. He liked the church. What a wonderful thing it was, a relief, a place to start over. The best part was that he could go to confession and wash away all the sins he had committed since his last confession. Sometimes he would catch the opening of the Saturday confessions and then come back two hours later to confess again some new small sins that had tripped him up in the interval. He was, when young, exceedingly fond of absolution.

He would enter the confessional—maybe three feet square, the smell of polished wood mixed with the stale incense from the last High Mass and the smoke from the candles—and he'd get on his knees on the kneeler and hear the click as the switch under the kneeler alerted the priest, and he'd know that the same switch lit the tiny red bulb over the door, so the next person in line wouldn't inadvertently come in during the middle of his confession. It smelled insanely religious in there, like nowhere else on earth, saturated with the fragrance of the blessed, just a hint of the metallic, a suggestion of decay, the scent of the priest.

Absolution was a wonder, worth everything Catholic. The

sweetest idea imaginable. But much later in his life Vaughn confessed to a college priest who said he would withhold absolution if Vaughn was just going to go out and sin again—get drunk, or screw some girl, or cheat on a test. There's one in every crowd, was Vaughn's thought. His fucking job was to sit there and deliver the forgiveness, the asshole.

After that religion was like, Who needs it?

Vaughn adored the Church, but only the lovely, forgiving Church in his head.

The storms on television looked wonderful. As a child all he wanted to do in storms was get outside, feel the rain, listen to the thunder, drown himself in it. He would take the dog and go sit in a big cardboard box in the yard, a box from a dishwasher or refrigerator. He did that all the time. The sound of water on cardboard still thrilled him. He had given up sitting in the yard in a cardboard box; but now, watching this hurricane show, he wondered why.

On TV, hurricanes meant dopey announcers at high-rise hotels. Vaughn didn't blame them for wanting to see what it felt like to be knocked around by hundred-mile-per-hour winds, he blamed them for doing it on TV. And he was jealous, too. And he figured they knew they were just doing what everybody else wanted to do.

As coast people understood, hurricanes were pretty before they were anything else. They usually didn't do much harm. They cleaned things out, knocked over some extra trees, ripped up some cheesy gas stations and old shacks. They were a thrill not otherwise available. They were big and they shook the house, the glass in the windows bent, things flew around. It was exciting to watch, to go out driving around when the rain was so thick you couldn't see a thing. There would be poles down in the street, wind gusts that could lift a man up off the ground, trees cracked thirty feet in the air, awnings ripped off buildings, roofs, too, gas station overhangs twisted like aluminum foil, glass storefronts shattered open, the guts of carwash places blown out—it was great stuff. And the residents were all in their houses with duct tape or plywood on the windows and the bathtubs filled with faucet water, with candles and more candles, flashlights and extra batteries, jars of peanut butter on the kitchen cabinet, store cakes, and chips and ice in the freezer compartment of the refrigerator that was soon to lose power, and bags of M&M's, books to read if things got slow, bread, and maybe hams—storm provisions.

Coast people knew all about it, they had been through it so often; and finally, though it was a little scary, it was still a pleasure to be alive and in the middle of it when the storm bruised up the sky, the light went shadowy, the world turned unearthly colors—green sky, lemon sky—as the storm swirled in, wreaked havoc on a scale that excited, like some fantasy monster, a benevolent and enormous wash cycle, howling into the night, screeching metal torn, any hinged thing banging endlessly, electrical lines snapping and shooting sparks into the weather's rage. And the natives got the best seats in the house.

It made static wonders of the world seem trifling. At least until you had one like Katrina, a killer, a storm of such power that everyone in its path went instantly from excitement to fear, fun to horror. Katrina had been the first hurricane of that sort he'd experienced up close, and the experience had tempered his ardor.

Vaughn and Gail had ridden out Katrina in the big brick house and come away unscathed, but the experience had been terrifying. The noise alone was enough to provide a constant threat of tragedy. Like standing next to a speeding train, everyone said, and that was close. It felt as if the place would fly apart, collapse at any moment, trees bent ninety degrees, ripped by winds, debris sailing by nonstop, catching momentarily in tree limbs, on twisted street signs, fire hydrants, half-toppled chimneys. Limbs whacking the house and the roof, shooting by when torn off their trunks. Most of the glass in the house was covered with half-inch plywood, screwed to the window frames, but on the east and west ends of the house, in a few places where the windows were protected by structure, Vaughn had used duct tape, and the open glass there gave them a frightening view of the storm. The constancy of it, the blow-your-house-down constancy. Once it got to them—their house was several miles inland, and well-east of landfall—it beat at the house for hours, with only a short respite in the middle as what must have been the edge of the eye passed nearby. When Katrina was done, and the morning light came, the destruction was mind-numbing. Even in Vaughn's inland-protected and fortunately located development the force of the storm was extraordinary. The area looked as if it had been strafed. Two houses on Tilted Tree Lane were opened up at their roofs. Trees were down on three others, and sixty-foot pines were strewn like pickup sticks on the ground, on cars, on the roofs and sides of houses—some snapped only feet off the ground, some snapped thirty feet in the air. And the confetti of tree limbs, leaves, pine cones, bicycles, plastic sheeting, shutters, plywood sheets, mailboxes, tangled wires, bags, clothing, framed pictures, shingles, lumber, tin roof vents, windshield wipers, hoses—the sight was jaw-dropping. Neighbors came out and walked around in stunned silence.

People asked one another how they were and the answer always came back a shrug, as if no one knew how he was, no one could actually say.

The people in his neighborhood cleaned up pretty quick, and things got back to normal, though they were without utilities for a couple of weeks. There was a lot of generator noise in the neighborhood, and people driving far and wide to get gas to run the generators—you had to go up to Interstate 10, or worse. But the weeks after the storm were a mixed time—relief to have made it through all right, stunned disbelief at the extent of the damage across the coast. Everything stopped. It was as if they were suddenly back in the nineteen-forties. Every day had time for no more than two projects—getting gasoline for the generator and finding ice. Or setting up an outdoor shower with the hose and a tarp after the water came back, and helping a neighbor remove a pine tree from the street. And it was hot. Gail and Vaughn spent a lot of time together. All conveniences were gone; they showered in the yard, pissed off the deck in the dark of night, shit on paper towels on the bathroom floor and packaged the result in Ziploc storage bags as if that were a likely adult diaper disposal system. It was hot. They slept in the living room with the doors to the deck wide open. When they used the generator they ran box fans, targeted at the bed.

When they got a chance they tried to drive the beach highway, but the Marines were there and they weren't keen on gawkers. The destruction closer to the beach was, as best they could see, total. A-bomb stuff. Like nothing they'd ever seen before.

———

Gail was in the room for a few minutes before he noticed that she was there. "What's this?" she said, pointing at the TV.

"Hurricanes," he said. "You guys back?"

"Is there a hurricane?" she said.

"No. This is *about* hurricanes."

He got up, kissed her on the cheek, went through the kitchen to the garage to see if there was something he could carry inside. She followed him.

Greta was in the garage using the bug killer to spray her car. "Ants," she said as he opened the door. "We've got ants. We're spraying the car. What've you been doing?"

"Watching TV. Praying," he said.

"There he goes again," Gail said, waving a hand at Greta asking for the spray can.

"Yeah, I'm unstoppable," Vaughn said.

"What're you praying *for*?" Greta asked.

"He just prays for no reason," Gail said. "It's a Catholic thing, I think. Sometimes he does it without even knowing he's doing it. We used to sit and watch TV and sometimes I'd catch him moving his lips, you know? He was saying Hail Marys."

"She's got me now," Vaughn said.

"That's new to me," Greta said. "Does it do any good?"

"Dunno," Vaughn said. "I'm just, like, saying old prayers I learned as a kid."

"Those are the best kind," Greta said.

"Amen," Gail said. She was shooting bug spray up under the dashboard. It was kind of hard to breathe there in the garage.

16

At mid-week they were all in the kitchen when Eddie arrived with Monkey. "I brought him over because he seemed lonely over at the place," he said.

"He's not the only one," Greta said.

"I make no bones about it," Eddie said. "I'm not afraid of my vulnerability. There isn't much going on over there when you guys are over here all the time."

Gail seemed to be talking to Newton a lot on the telephone. Now they'd taken up text-messaging each other. It was annoying—her cell made this little squirting noise when she sent a message and then she would be giggling at the tiny screen, then thumb-typing for ten more minutes just to say "Cnt tlk. At mov. Cll U ltr."

"Why don't you either talk to him or e-mail him? This text stuff is ridiculous," Vaughn said.

"Chill, Vaughn," she said. "We like to text."

"Great," he said.

"Eddie, why don't you come visit me in my room where I am going to be folding warm clothes just out of the dryer," Greta said.

"We'll take Monkey," Gail said. "We're going for a walk."

Vaughn got up from the kitchen table and took the leash from Eddie. "Thanks," he said.

When Vaughn and Gail got outside it was cool, more than usually cool. The sun was almost down and the light had that quiet look about it. He gave her the leash and they walked down the street.

"I had an idea," Gail said.

"What?" he said.

"What if we went ahead and got married again? In a church this time? It might put something back into the marriage, something that's been missing for a while. Something I can't put my finger on."

"Probably not," Vaughn said.

"I think it would help me settle down," she said.

"You seem pretty settled down already."

"I have trouble keeping things straight in my head," she said. "A new marriage sanctified by the Church would help me keep everything in order."

"I don't like marriage anymore," he said. "It screws everybody up."

"No," she said. "Or maybe it's the other way around?"

For some reason Monkey decided to bow up and do his business right in the middle of the road. Vaughn looked around to see if any of the neighbors were watching.

"What's that about?" Gail said.

"I've never seen him do that before," Vaughn said.

"We'd better get it," she said.

He headed back to the house for a shovel. He didn't know what to make of her proposition. Was she dreaming? Did she not *get* Greta? It was crazy talk, really. Just after the divorce he could have imagined it, but now? Or did she see something in his connection to Greta that told her he wasn't that intrigued? It was true Vaughn was not swept away by Greta, but it was also true that he did not see himself as likely to be swept away by anyone. The time for *swept away* was too long gone, replaced by a constellation of smaller, less vibrant, slower pleasures. Greta was low-key, easy-does-it, no maintenance, pleasant to be around, took care of herself—a nice woman. They had gotten something started against the odds, and he wasn't in any hurry to shut it down. Still, Gail's crackball suggestions unnerved him, put him to thinking about what he was doing, apart from saving his ex. He had been so busy splitting up with her for the last year that he hadn't thought so much about what the future held with Greta. And with Gail, he wasn't sure what would happen if he just said one day that she ought to move on, that they were never getting back together. He'd tried to say it lots of ways, but Gail wasn't quite listening, or at least she appeared to not quite listen. It was impossible to gauge how she might react to such directness. It might be a stark, harsh rebuke, throwing her into crying jags, more depression, more coming-apart-at-the-seams party nights; it might be the tonic that was needed. There was no way to know. His own personal reality show.

In the time since the move, Vaughn had looked at Gail and Greta, trying to see them afresh, even when he knew this wasn't a healthy project. He watched the ways they moved, how they talked, how they walked, sat, smiled. Often they seemed to be mimicking each other, even to the point of being one person in two bodies. They liked each other far too much for the circumstance. They picked up each other's gestures, remarks, asides just because of the proximity, he guessed. But they did it so effortlessly that it may have been something more. At close range they weren't, after all, as different as they might seem. He listened to them, their jokes, their affections and reprimands. He watched the ways they walked, the ways they treated their forearms and wrists, how they held their hands, how they placed their knees when sitting, what they did with their feet, how they moved their hair with their hands, facial expressions made with the eyes and mouth, cheeks and eyebrows—they became more alike every day.

He hadn't told Greta that Gail had brought up getting re-married a week before. He figured it for some momentary lapse. Now, the repeated proposal had an awkward realness.

They got Monkey's trouble cleaned up and headed inside. Eddie and Greta were watching TV, a murder documentary about a Christian polygamist who had killed one of his wives and sawed her teeth out and cut off her fingers so that she would not be identified if discovered.

"I don't think we ought to be watching this," Vaughn said.

"It's *American Justice*," Eddie said.

"We're keeping up with modern crime," Greta said.

" 'Why?' the detective said, his eyebrows lifting remotely," Vaughn said.

"Hmm," Greta said. "He has a point." She clicked off the TV and patted Eddie's shoulder. "Time to motor on," she said. "Monkey needs to get home."

The party broke up just like that. Eddie departed without

another word. Gail said good night and retired to her bedroom. Vaughn and Greta repaired to the kitchen for ice cream and cake.

She said, "You look like something's bothering you."

"Look at you," he said.

"What?"

"No. I mean, yes. Something's going on. I think the whole game is going off the rails. Gail says she wants to get remarried. In the Church, she said."

"Whoops," Greta said.

"She said something last week, but I thought it was—I don't know—some kind of wouldn't-it-be-lovely moment."

"Remarriage something you're interested in?" Greta said.

"Probably not," he said. "But it makes things harder."

"Well," Greta said, carving some icing off the cake they'd uncovered on the kitchen table. "You're a popular guy."

"Thanks, Vernon."

"She has a weakness for you," Greta said.

"Maybe," he said. "Maybe she's just thinking backward. All we have to do is turn her around face front and she'll be totally repaired."

He cut himself a ridiculously large slice of cake and toppled it over on its side on his plate. Then he realized it was way too big and tried to cut it horizontally, from the middle of the broad outside arc toward the pointed edge of the wedge. That wasn't working too well when Greta took the knife out of his hand.

"Let a cake girl do this, will you?" she said.

"I can't believe she's serious," Vaughn said. "I mean, she's just talking, isn't she? Bored, alone, as tired as the rest of us. Just wants a friend. Think about it that way, you can't blame her." He wagged his fork at Greta. "Her idea is you can stay, too. Even Eddie. We become the Addams Family."

"Probably not going to happen," Greta said.

"Why do we bother to do any of this?" he said. "I mean, we do stuff and you know up front it's not going to work. I guess we're just passing time, waiting for her to get better, or waiting for things to change. Reminds me of my father."

"Dead, you mean?"

"Cute," he said. "No. I was thinking half-smart. He played the system to make a career. Taught me to do that. I was supposed to be this designer and what I really did was steal stuff and paste it together. I guess you gotta have an eye for what to steal. Then turn it on its ear and present it with authority. Not rocket science. Roughly the equivalent of wearing funny clothes."

"I would have liked your father, I think."

"He was okay. He wasn't a genius, or a hero, but he wasn't bad. There's something to be said for knowing, even belatedly, your limitations."

"True that," she said.

"My father taught me stuff, all kinds of things—taught me about tools, drawings, pencils, and later, about getting jobs, how to hold a woman while dancing. He taught me all this stuff, but it was peculiar, an odd mix. There was, for him, always an ideal form. Every act, every gesture, every remark, everything could eventually be discovered in its ideal state through focus and study."

"You're lucky, then." Greta got the ice cream back out of the freezer and dished herself another scoop. "You want one?" she asked, pointing at Vaughn with the pink plastic ice cream scoop.

"He had studied many things and had already discovered the ideal forms," Vaughn said. "I, on the other hand, had a lot of bad haircuts. My father took pictures of every one of them, a chronicle of constant errors."

"That wasn't so nice of him. Maybe he was just fond of taking pictures of you? I mean, that's another possible explanation, isn't it?"

"Hey, I never thought of that."

"Fuck you very much," she said, smiling.

"I don't know," Vaughn said. "I'm feeling poorly about myself and my fellow creatures. This deal *seems* easy, but it's a tiny nightmare for me, and I'm thinking a nightmare for you, too, and for Gail, well, her three."

"People make errors," Greta said. "They find out later. It's fine."

"I wish I was a better architect," he said. "I always liked the art end of the business, peculiar architects who did peculiar things. It seemed possible to make a world that provided psychological beauty and stability sufficient to guide the user, or to counterbalance the effects of others. When I was in school my stuff was erratic. I was the patch-it-together guy. Got that from my instructors, I guess, before they fell off the planet. Ad hoc–ism, or something. Worked great when combined with haughty one-upmanship. Lo and behold, soon I was the hero student."

"And the rest is history," Greta said. She yawned and collected the plates, bowls, plastic silverware, rinsed everything in the sink and placed the pieces in the dishwasher.

"You don't have to rinse them for this dishwasher," Vaughn said. "Gail demonstrated that for me once. It's in the manual."

"Got you coming and going, huh? You ready for bed?"

"So anyway, I had a long and profitable career. Heady days, until I couldn't stand it anymore. I quit the last place, moved to the coast, took small jobs for local architects—just drawing, a skill that I finally mastered. I didn't do design. I was just that weird guy who drew pretty well."

She tugged on his arm, pulling him out of the chair. "And you faked them out for a really long time, is that it?"

"I guess," Vaughn said.

"And you're a bad person, and your dad, well, he was, as they say, a dream. I see where you're going with this, Vaughn. And it's *really* maudlin. You got maudlin written all over you. You're rolling in maudlin, dripping with it. You gotta stop. You're lucky I've got a high tolerance, you know? Normal woman would've slapped you silly a half hour ago."

"Yeah yeah," he said. "Bite me."

"I don't know," she said, reaching for his hand to lead him from the room. "You might get lucky. You might trick me."

17

Tony showed up in the front yard in the middle of the night Saturday with a garden hoe and a pickup truck the size of a tank. He was yelling for Gail to come out and talk to him. Gail was in her room—maybe she was asleep, maybe she was awake. Vaughn didn't know which. It was very late. He went out on the balcony outside his room and said, "Who are you and what do you want?"

"I'm Tony," Tony said. "And I want to see Gail. Who're you?"

"I'm her husband."

"Oh," Tony said. "I didn't know she had a husband."

"Yeah, she does, and it's me," Vaughn said.

"You were out of town," he said.

"I've been out of town awhile. About a year."

"Well, tell her I want to talk to her, will you?"

"She's asleep," Vaughn said. He thought he probably should have said she wasn't there, but he wasn't thinking that clearly.

"Wake her up?" Tony said.

"I'm not going to wake her up. What the fuck do you want anyway?"

"You want to start something with me?" Tony said.

"It's the middle of the night and you're in my front yard with a truck. You want me to call the cops? What're you doing here?"

"I'm her boyfriend," Tony said.

"You're her boyfriend?" Vaughn said. "That the same boyfriend who beat the crap out of her a while back?"

"Nothing like that," Tony said. "I guess I need to talk to you, if you're her husband."

"I don't want to talk to you," Vaughn said. "I want to go back to sleep."

"Is she right there?" Tony said. He pointed at Vaughn.

"No, she's not here. She's in the other room. I just came out here to see who was yelling."

It was one of those chilly nights, wispy sky was moving fast. There were a few stars behind the clouds. Dogs were barking in the distance. Vaughn could hear the cars out on the coast road.

"What's with the hoe?" he said.

"What?" Tony said.

"The garden tool," Vaughn said. "The hoe."

Tony looked at it as if he'd forgotten he had it in his hand. He was leaning on it, sort of like that painting. "I don't know," he said. "I just had it in the truck. I was hoeing some stuff earlier."

Vaughn nodded and wiped his eyes, rubbing them with

his thumb and index finger, squeezing the bridge of his nose. "Well, can you call tomorrow?" he said.

"What?" he said.

"Call tomorrow," Vaughn said and turned to go inside.

"Whoa, wait a minute," Tony said. "We need to talk."

"We don't," Vaughn said.

"We do," Tony said. "You got me all wrong. Come on down, will you?"

Vaughn was guessing at his easiest path out. Was it call the police or go inside and hope Tony would leave? Tony didn't look like a guy who was going to leave.

"Just get out," Vaughn said. "Go on home. Come back when you're sober."

"I'm sober now. I want to talk to you. I think we'd better have a conversation."

"What about?"

"Her," he said.

Vaughn looked up at the sky. The moon was almond-shaped, like a person's eye. He couldn't figure it. He motioned toward the back door. "I'll be down in a minute," he said. "Put away your weapon and get the truck out of the yard."

Tony wanted a beer and Vaughn gave him one and they sat together at the kitchen table. The kitchen was spotless, the way it usually was. The beer was Mexican. Tony looked at the label and chuckled. "No shit," he said.

Vaughn sized the kid up. Vaughn was bigger than him by half a foot, but Tony looked fit and strong. He might have been thirty, soaking wet. Vaughn figured if it came to that, he could probably cool Tony just by wrapping him up and hus-tling him out the door; but if the kid started swinging, Vaughn was going to get hit. He figured Tony didn't really want to get into a fight. Sometimes it happens, but more often than not, even if the guy doesn't want to admit it, he is looking for a way out. Vaughn could make that work for him.

"So what's the deal with you and her?" Tony said.

"We're married. We've been married for a hundred years. Sometimes we live apart, sometimes we live together. Right now we're living together. Since that show you put on a few weeks ago, you're not really welcome around here."

"She started it," he said.

"I don't care who started it," Vaughn said.

"She hit me right here with a beer can," he said. He drew his hand along his cheekbone, alongside his left eye.

"She could have hit you with a hoe, for all I care," Vaughn said. "You beat the shit out of her."

"Did not. I didn't beat her. I just pushed her around a little bit," Tony said. He did a long tug on his beer. "She fell down a couple times."

"You guys," Vaughn said. "We went to the hospital."

Tony looked at him for a minute, sort of looking past the neck of his beer, and said, "So that's when you came back, right?" And he smiled.

It was Vaughn's turn to scratch at the beer bottle. He did that for a minute, watching his fingernail cut the label. "Yeah, well, maybe you've got me there, Tony," he said. "But I've been here every day since."

"Who's the other woman?" he said.

"What other woman?"

"The other one. You know," he said. "The other one I always see you leaving with."

Vaughn watched the second hand on the clock, thinking it had been a long time since he'd been in a situation like this. He was trying to figure out which one of them was ahead. Tony seemed plenty docile, so that was points for Vaughn. On the other hand, Tony had made it into the kitchen, which was big for him. If he made a break for the door into the rest of the house, Vaughn would have to hit him with a chair, he figured. He looked at the chair—where would he grab it?

"She's an old friend of ours," he said.

"She is?" Tony said. "What about the guy over on Mary Magdalene?"

"Yeah, he's a friend, too," Vaughn said. "Eddie. His name's Eddie. Greta stays over there sometimes. Sometimes she stays over here. It just depends."

"He's only got one hand," Tony said. "That Eddie. How'd he lose it? The hand?"

"Desert Storm," Vaughn said. "What do you care? You've been following us around a lot, have you? That's not exactly legal. That's not exactly the smart thing to do after what happened with you and Gail, is it? Police might be interested in hearing about you."

"Police, schmolice," Tony said. "You aren't calling any police."

"I did last time, didn't I?"

"You didn't. She did," he said, pointing up into the house. "I know what goes on. She told me. She told me everything."

"Oh yeah? When was that?" Vaughn said.

"I see her," he said. "When I want to, when she wants to.

She comes by. We see each other. We're grown-ups. What, that's news to you?"

Vaughn shrugged. Tony was ahead by more than he'd figured.

It wasn't too bright there in the kitchen. There wasn't much light. The only lights on were the ones over the stove and over the sink. There were lots of shadows. From outside there were tree shadows on the glass. Vaughn got the feeling he'd made a pretty big mistake letting Tony into the house. He got the feeling he ought to get him out of the house, if he could.

"Here's the deal," Vaughn said. "We've got an arrangement. We've got a deal, so you can do whatever you want. But we're not doing it tonight. Okay? Tonight you're finishing the beer and going home."

"You giving me orders?"

"No," Vaughn said, sighing. "I'm not giving you orders. I'm suggesting in the nicest possible way that maybe the best thing we could do, the best thing *you* could do right at this moment, is finish that beer and walk out the door."

"Then what?" he said.

"Whatever you want," Vaughn said. "This house is going to sleep."

"What about us?" he said.

By this time Vaughn was making big gestures every which way. He realized that the gestures were *too* big. He was shrugging and holding his hand up in the air and making faces, rubbing his hand over his scalp. He was clearly at a loss. Tony couldn't miss it.

"What about us?" Vaughn said, turning his head and squinting a little.

"What's this deal you've got with her? You're living here, she's living here, she's going out with me—what kind of deal is that?"

"She's not doing too well," he said. "She's not feeling so well in the world. She's suffered some discontinuities, if you know what I mean. Things aren't quite going her way."

"That includes you?" Tony said.

Vaughn shook his head. "I don't know," he said, his voice going slower and deeper, quieter. The kind of voice you use when you're really getting tired of the game, playing up the menace. Even he thought it was funny.

"What're you laughing at?" Tony said.

"Nothing," he said. "I just thought of something."

"What?" he said.

"It's nothing," Vaughn said. "You leaving or what? I'm going up to bed."

"You're going to let me stay here in the kitchen?" he said.

"No, you're not staying in the kitchen, Tony. I want you to get in your truck and go home and do what you do. Do it out of sight."

"Oh, that's pretty," he said.

"What can I say? You trashed her and now you're seeing her on the sly or whatever. She's upset. She's having some kind of breakdown. I'm trying to cover the goddamn thing, and here you are at three in the fucking morning in the front yard. I mean, for Christ's sake, can you get a clue here and back out?"

"Whoa," Tony said.

"Yeah, that's right," Vaughn said. "Whoa."

"Tough guy," he said.

"It's not about tough guy. It's about being tired and having had enough. You know what I mean? Whatever you want to do is fine with me. Whatever she wants to do is fine with me. Whatever the two of you want to do together is fine with me. But if she turns up hurt, it's not fine with me. That's why I'm here and why I'm going to stay here. That's why you're not staying here. And that's about what I've got."

Tony scratched his forehead as if he was thinking. "Well," he finally said, "that makes some sense. You know what I mean?" He looked at Vaughn earnestly. "That makes a lot of sense. You make a lot of sense." He looked at him again. "Tell me, are you a lot older than she is?"

"Some," he said.

"You look older," Tony said.

"Thanks," Vaughn said.

Tony tipped the bottle up and drained it, put it on the middle of the kitchen table, stood up, pushed the chair back in gently. "The power of persuasion," he said.

"Ain't it something."

He smiled at Vaughn and held out a hand, and Vaughn took it and shook it, and then led Tony to the kitchen door, and Tony strode out like a gentleman.

Gail was sitting on the upstairs landing playing with a tiny electric train set she had bought Vaughn for his birthday one year. It was N-gauge tiny; the tracks were about a quarter inch apart; the cars were about two inches long. She had a little circle built, and she was running the train around in the circle. She had the red and silver engine, a boxcar, a flat car, a tanker car, and a little half-size caboose. She was watching the train go around this twenty-four-inch circle. She was driving it real slow.

"So what'd he want?" she said.

"I guess you already know that."

"What, are you mad at me or something?"

"Mad doesn't get it," he said.

"You need to save me from myself."

"I'm beginning to understand that," Vaughn said.

"It's shitty of you to have brought that woman in here," she said.

"I thought you were okay with that woman," he said.

"Yeah, I'm sure you did," she said. She sped the train up and it went around one more time and then flew off the track. A problem he recognized. "You just brought her here to protect you."

"Gail, it's like the middle of the night and I've just had your boyfriend for cookies in the kitchen, and I was thinking we ought to just let this go and maybe talk about it tomorrow."

"You're mad at me because I've been seeing Tony," she said.

"I'm not mad at you. If you want to see Tony, that's your business," he said. "He's about half your age."

"Like that matters," she said.

"He's about half your IQ," he said.

"Like *that* matters," she said.

"So, nothing matters, then," he said. "I'm going to turn in."

"I need you to stay here and talk to me," she said. "Sit down, will you?"

She was putting the train back on the tracks. It was difficult. She had to get the front wheels on the track, all four of them, then she had to get the back wheels on the track, and then she had to scoot the car back and forth to be sure it was on the track, and then she had to put the next car on and had to bump it into the first car in order to hook them up, and she didn't have a lot of patience. Pretty soon she had the engine dragging the cars around half on and half off the track. He motioned at the train. "Turn it off, will you." He got down on his hands and knees and put on his reading glasses and tried to get the cars right.

Gail said, "I don't know what it is, I just like him."

"He's a real man," he said.

"Boy," she said.

"Whatever," he said. "Whatever he is, he's real."

"He's simple. That's what he is," she said. "That's what makes him attractive. I think I'll probably get rid of him soon."

"I think you probably won't," he said. "But it's all right as long as he doesn't beat you up again. You can see whoever you want."

"I guess I can," she said, and she sped the train up and ran it off the tracks again. "Why'd you leave me?" she said.

He shook his head and picked up the engine, flipped a finger at the wheels. "I don't know. You asked me to. That's the way I remember it."

"Yeah," she said, "but you know—"

"Yeah, I know," he said.

"I figured it was just time. Something wasn't right," she said.

"You were mad at me, but I couldn't figure out why," he said.

"I wasn't mad so much as tired of you," she said.

He handed her the little engine. "That could be too much candor," he said.

"There's a time for candor," she said.

"This isn't it," he said.

"Apparently," she said.

Just about then a door opened down the hall and Greta walked out in a pair of shorts and one of his shirts. She was coming out of his bedroom. She was buttoning the shirt. She looked down the hall and saw them sitting there in front of Gail's room, and she said, "Well, howdy-do. And good night." Then she turned around and started to go into her room.

"Come on out," Gail said. "Come out and play."

"We're playing trains," Vaughn said.

Greta kept one hand on the doorjamb, stood for a moment in the hall and said, "You guys go on. I just wanted to see what happened with the guy in the truck."

"Vaughn took care of him," Gail said. "Sent him packing."

"Oh," Greta said. "Well, you guys carry on. I'm going in here to read or bathe or sleep. Probably all those things. It's going to take me an hour or two. Could take me all night."

Gail looked at Greta, then at him. "What does that mean?" she said.

Greta waved. "It doesn't mean anything. I'm going." She did another odd wave and shut the door behind her.

"That went well," he said.

"This whole thing's gone well," she said. "From the very first. The two of you coming over, taking up residence. It's very yesterday, isn't it?"

"I don't know what you expected me to do," he said. "I'm living with this woman and what—you want me to come over here and leave her?"

"It's a thought," Gail said.

"Not happening. We split up. You wanted me out of here as fast as you could get me out of here."

"That's not true," she said.

"Is," he said.

"Well, it may have been true for a while, but it wasn't *completely* true."

"It was pretty true," he said.

"It wasn't permanent, though," she said.

"Sometimes things don't start out to be permanent but end up that way."

"What's that, a Hallmark card?" she said.

"This is tough stuff," he said. "All of it."

"You've got that right," she said. "We were married. We were married a long time. We had a life. Maybe we should have stayed together. Maybe that's what we were supposed to do."

"Tried that," he said.

"Why are you such a fucking smartass all the time?" she said. "*Tried that.* How's that make me feel when you say something like that?"

"I'm only telling you the truth," he said.

"I'm fucking naked as a fucking baby out here, and you're saying *Tried that,*" she said.

"What can I say?" he said. "I'm not happy either. I wasn't happy about it when I left. I wasn't happy about it when I was living out there by myself. It was all about you. Then it sort of changed."

"What changed?" she said.

"The whole deal. You got to be more trouble than, you know. It was too much trouble."

"Oh, good," she said. "So what am I now?"

"I don't know," he said. "You are what you are. Ex. Wife, partner, lover. Friend, pal, buddy. What's anybody? Know what I mean?"

"No, I do not know what you mean," she said. "What *do* you mean?"

"After a while, what's anybody you hang out with, go to dinner with, drive around with, do errands with, go to movies with? Anybody you make things for—drinks, coffee, you know? A member of your operation."

"Are you sliding around the question?"

"I'm trying to," he said. He moved over so he was leaning against the wall, sitting on the floor and leaning against the wall next to her. Their shoulders were touching. He could smell her and she smelled the way she had always smelled, kind of lovely and vaguely perfumed. A scent of some soap that wasn't too fancy but that smelled good anyway. The old scent. They watched some lights stretch across the windows in front of the house. She started disassembling the train set. He stopped her.

"Leave it together," he said.

"Yeah?" she said.

"Put it on a table somewhere. We'll run it later."

"I don't know how this is going to end up," she said. "Is it going to get worse?"

"Might turn out fine," he said.

"I wish you liked me more," she said.

"Not fair," he said.

"I apologize," she said. "And I do sort of like her. Greta, I mean. I do and I don't."

"Figured that," he said.

"Are you in love with her?" she said.

"I don't think that's happening anymore," he said. "That love thing. Or maybe it just changed clothes and I don't recognize it."

"I shouldn't have asked," she said.

"It doesn't hurt anything," he said. He was looking at some lights out the window. "Sometimes it's better just to go ahead and say stuff."

Porch light was throwing shadows through the glass upstairs across from the landing. A Palladian window, the house description said. As if after Palladio who, had he seen it, would have rolled over in his grave. The light coming through this arched window made a shadow like some kind of bat—big eyes, big ears. A strange shadow. He pointed it out to Gail and said, "You see this over here?"

"What?" she said.

"Here," he said. He touched her shoulder to guide her.

"Oh, yeah. I've seen that thing before," she said. "He lives here."

He put his arm around Gail and pulled her toward him, kissed her temple, smelled her hair. They stayed there a few minutes, just breathing. It wasn't too bad. After a while she got up, patted Vaughn on the shoulder, and went into her room, leaving the train set in the hall. Vaughn stayed put for a minute, listened to her light switch snap, then got up and went down the hall and stood by Greta's door. Not a sound.

18

Vaughn woke up at about eleven in the morning with Gail sitting on the bed alongside him and poking his neck gently with the tip of a pink, resin-coated Japanese carving knife he had bought her a couple of years before. "Morning, darling," she said.

"Uh-huh," he said. "I see. How are you?"

"I think you're going to love me," Gail said, making motions as if to gently slice his throat. "I can be dangerous, too."

"Too playful," he said. "Besides, I already loved you."

She put the knife under his ear, slid it down as if cutting his throat, a sawing motion from left ear to right. "Yeah, but you stopped," she said.

"I didn't stop," he said. "I just got old or something. I went on sabbatical. You want to get off me here? I gave you this knife, you know."

"You remember," she said.

"Jump up, will you?"

"I guess," she said, rolling away from him. She held the knife out at arm's length and tried to get some light on it. "It's pretty, don't you think?"

"It's prettier there than on my neck," he said. "It's prettiest in the catalog."

"I would never hurt you, Vaughn," she said. "What would be the percentage in that?"

"I don't know—Gail works in mysterious ways?"

"She certainly does," Gail said. "I talked to your brother this morning. I asked him to come down and see us. I said he was needed here."

"Tell me this is another joke."

"He said if I needed him he will come," she said.

"That's all we need," he said. "Little Newton."

"Not so little," Gail said.

By now she was on her back lying in the bed next to him. He sat up, smacking some shape into his pillow.

"About Tony," she said. "I like him, he likes me. He's fun. He's dumb enough for both of us. I like a dumb guy." She turned her head on the pillow to look at Vaughn. "A dumb guy is a significant asset these days. He thinks the world of me."

"As he should," he said. "He's nineteen and you are a legendary sex goddess."

"I hear that," she said. "But when they're young and dumb, they're young and . . ."

"Dumb," he said. "What are the virtues of dumb again?"

"He's not really dumb. He's more like . . . ill-informed."

"I don't like him," Vaughn said.

"Noted," she said.

"Does he have a job?" he said.

"I don't think so," she said. "He does tree work sometimes. He's a hanger guy."

"What's a hanger guy?" he said.

"The guy who goes up in a tree and cuts out the little pieces that have broken off but are still hanging up there."

"No kidding? They've got a name for that?" Vaughn said.

She nodded and sat up on her side of the bed, crossed her legs and faced him. "Newton is coming. I told him to come."

"Well, shit, Gail. Where's he staying? Here? If he's coming, we're going back to Greta's."

"No, you're staying here," she said. "He's staying here. Greta can stay, too. If you must have her close by."

Vaughn gave her an eye-roll.

"Jerry Colonna," she said, getting out of the bed. "See? I remembered." She twirled the knife in her hand, then tried tossing it at the floor to see if she could stick it mumblety-peg style. It bounced. "Why don't you get up and we'll go out," she said. "Get your friend and the three of us will go somewhere."

They went to Target. Target was full of young girls wearing blue jeans that made their butts look like they didn't fit in the jeans. Made their butts waddle as they walked. He pointed this out to Greta who said, "Keep looking, Bozo."

"It's the rage," Gail said. "I'm thinking about going that way."

"This is a post-slice-of-stomach thing?"

"The stomach is still present, you will notice," Greta said.

She pointed out a girl in jeans and a short top walking by. The girl was pretty. Her stomach was pretty. Her butt looked like it was too large for the jeans, but it was still pretty.

"They want you to look at their butts," Gail said. "Well—not you, but, you know."

"What are we doing here?" Vaughn said.

"We're having a ménage," Gail said. "A relationship. The three of us. We're turning over a new leaf. We're making a new start. We're keeping me away from Tony, and we're getting an iPod. All those things."

"Gail wants an iPod," Greta said.

"Then she shall have an iPod even if every right-thinking individual of sound mind in these United States deplores the iPod utterly," he said.

"Whoa," Gail said. "I want one I can put all my music on."

"Game, set, match," he said. "You've got no music."

"I do, too," she said. "I remember music from before your time. Before you I was a woman who loved music. Then you married me and took my music away. You made me feel so bad about loving music that I never listened to music again. But now I'm going to listen to music all day and all night on my iPod."

"Got it," Vaughn said.

They went through the bra section where all the bras looked like car bumpers, big rose and blue car bumpers. "In my day," he said, pointing at the brassieres.

"We know, we know," Greta said.

"Nipples," Gail said. "Nipples be gone."

"What a world," he said.

"That's one of his favorite expressions," Gail said to Greta.

"I know," Greta said. "He uses it when he means to draw

166

attention to what he thinks is the extreme peculiarity of the way we live now, in this case as exemplified by women's undergarments."

"Right," Gail said.

"He's got a great deal of range," Greta said.

"He sees the world in a brassiere," Gail said.

Then they arrived at the iPod aisle. All things iPod were represented on this aisle. Actually, it was half an aisle, but it was all iPod all the time—sweaters, ear buds, earphones, cases, stands, speakers. All cute and all brightly colored. Many, many white. It was iPod World.

They looked at the iPods available and Greta and Gail were fascinated. They compared the iPods, one against the other— the size of the Shuffle and of the new Shuffle, and the size of the Nano and the size of the Mini, now long discontinued but still available in lime at this Target. Then they compared capacities—one hundred and twenty songs, two hundred and fifty songs, five hundred songs, thousands of songs.

"It's way too late to get an iPod," Vaughn said.

"We're older people now and we can get iPods whenever we damn well please," Greta said.

"Are you getting an iPod, too?"

"I might," she said. "Have you something against that?"

"I have something against it coming to rest in the closet two weeks from now," he said.

"Put it on eBay," she said. "If that even happens."

"Where are we going to lunch with our iPods after we get them?" Gail said.

"Chinese," he said.

"You always say that," Gail said. "He always says that," she said to Greta.

"I know," Greta said.

"Why don't we go to some real place," Gail said. "Like a delicatessen or some sandwich place."

"I'd like some Fritos," Greta said.

"You guys are too hard to please," Vaughn said.

"I invited his brother to come down," Gail said to Greta. "He doesn't like his brother. He thinks his brother is too something. What is it that you think your brother is?"

"Too short," he said.

"His brother's a walking man," Gail said. "He walks tall, all the time, night and day. Three o'clock in the morning and he's out walking tall."

"That could be dangerous," Greta said.

"It's good for his heart, though," Gail said. "What's-his-face here could use some of that. He's a little thick through the you-know-what."

"Skull?" Greta said.

"Let's get some Chinese food first," Vaughn said. "Sesame beef."

"What about this one?" Gail whispered, pointing out a young girl in lemon-colored, skin-tight knee-length stretch pants who came into the aisle talking on a cell phone and fingering the iPod accessories.

"*Naked Came the Stranger,*" he said.

"Could be a very attractive thong," Gail said.

"I'm going to the car," Vaughn said. He waved and walked out, leaving them there among the iPods. He didn't know why they were suddenly mad for iPods, why they were being so friendly to each other, why he and Greta were still at Gail's house. He didn't know why anything was happening, and what was happening seemed sort of out of control.

Most of all he was unhappy about Newton. He did not want to see Newton, did not want to endure Newton's smug face, Newton's half-thoughts, Newton's great success.

"Getting old is hell," he said to a woman his age who was going out the door of Target with him. She looked startled.

Vaughn was glad to get to the car, to climb inside, to click the seatbelt into place even though he was parked in the parking lot. He was glad to hear the door shut and to smell the interior—the leather. He was glad to touch the steering wheel, the shift knob, the radio buttons. He felt safe in the car. He felt protected. He watched the people in the parking lot and thought things about them. He thought: That one's pretty and that one shouldn't wear those pants, those three must be related, look at the way that one walks, that one sure is fat, she sure bought a lot of stuff, he's too tall, why are they laughing like that, that woman looks like a duck with those feet, I like her hair, he spits like a jerk, that one's too tucked-in for my taste, I wouldn't mind having a bite of that. He watched these people pack their bags into the backseats of their cars and get in and drive away, backing out of slots carefully and not so carefully. He watched the traffic. He watched the whole thing—the little breezes blowing the helpless trees, the tall solid lamp standards, the brick buildings, the giant red balls in front of the doors at Target, dividing the walkway from the roadway. He liked being in the car better than anything that had happened to him in days. He was thinking that maybe he should just go around and sit in parking lots in his car as much as possible. He wondered if he would get bored doing that, if the charm would wear off like it wore off everything else. He decided it probably would, but that there were alternatives, that he could go to a fast-food restaurant and get a hamburger if that happened, or to a frozen yogurt drive-thru, or another parking lot. There were many possibilities, he decided, enough to sustain him should the pleasures of this particular parking lot wane.

Out the windshield clouds clogged the sky. Big white, thick clouds looking like the world's intestines wrapped around themselves. He started the car and turned on the air conditioning, put it on low, leaned his head against the seat. Without looking, he reached for the switch to lock all the doors, pressed the button and heard the satisfying *thunk*. He listened to the muffled chatter and scratch of passersby—their feet on the asphalt, their voices rising and falling. He wondered if he would ever get out of this. And if so, then what? He wondered if a new dog would be a good idea. Maybe a cat named Frank who hunted at night and brought him field mice and cardinals. Why not marry her? he thought. Meaning Greta, he was pretty sure. Why fool around? Because he missed the past so much, all those other times, all those other moments, all those other things, places, and people, all those events. All that. There was so much *stuff* back there, behind him, now lost, vanished, but for that no less troubling. The world of distant memory. The world of the barely recalled, of a life that was like a movie he had lived in. A wonderful movie with weather and women, sparkling streets at night, tight embraces in dark, unrecognizable rooms. A world that now might just as well have never existed, but plagued him sorely.

He sat up, slid the gearshift into Drive, and drove across the parking lot diagonally, toward the Burger King.

Fifteen minutes later, having enjoyed a very satisfying and salty Whopper, Vaughn rolled back around to Target and found Gail and Greta standing out front. They'd been waiting there for him. They were both wearing white Apple ear buds, and they both had iPods strung around their necks. They looked like sisters.

19

It had taken Vaughn too long to figure out being a good architect and being a successful architect were two distinctly different things, and that getting his name and his buildings in the magazines was not going to bring him lasting satisfaction. He had spent the best part of his life working toward that, and had succeeded in some measure, in a regional way, among the architects and designers of Dallas and Atlanta; but as it became less important to him, he became a man with fewer ideas and opinions. At some point not too long ago he more or less gave up the pursuit and went into some kind of death spiral, dropping one job after another, slipping down the architectural food chain until he was detailing toilet stalls for a company that sold and installed them. That's when he stepped out entirely, went to the community colleges and offered his services, which were warmly received.

His brother, Newton, by contrast, was a believer. Success was available and real, true, honest, genuine, and fundamental. Good work was rewarded, poor work was scorned. Money was an accidental side-benefit. Newton was much more successful than Vaughn had ever been. Newton lived in Oregon and Seattle. Up there in the Great Northwest, as Newton had once called it. He started a small computer company working with secondary Internet searches, and he eventually sold the company to one of the big Internet search engines. As part of the deal, Newton now had a position with that company, or one of its subsidiaries, which didn't require him to do much of anything but deliver an occasional opinion about an idea produced by one of the company's one hundred design teams.

He and Newton had never been the best of friends, even as children, so he was not pleased when Newton showed up in Gulfport at Gail's invitation. Vaughn's view of his brother was poisoned by envy; Vaughn knew it, but was helpless to correct it. He didn't see eye to eye with Newton, never had. Newton was the family favorite; Vaughn was the black sheep. Newton was the successful one. Newton was in his time, while Vaughn was out of his. Vaughn believed his mother loved his brother more than she loved him, and his father made no secret of his preference for Newton. And there was the matter of Gail having been Newton's lover before she was Vaughn's. It was a short romance, only a month, or six weeks, but fierce and exciting for both of them before they called it quits.

So when Gail called Newton, Vaughn was displeased.

Newton hadn't ever visited Mississippi, and Vaughn only

spoke to Newton on holidays, the required calls. But now Newton was arriving at the airport and Vaughn was sent to fetch him.

Vaughn got to the airport with half an hour or more to spare. In the small terminal at Gulfport there was a tall young girl, maybe twenty-two or twenty-four. She was thin as a post, no breasts to speak of, no hips either. She walked funny, sort of on her tiptoes, swung her butt a little. Her hair was a delicious brown. She had clear, caramel-colored eyes. Without thinking, Vaughn started following this girl around the airport, walking behind her, or off to the side as inconspicuously as he could, which was not very inconspicuous in a terminal the size of a department store. They stopped at various concession spots—magazine kiosks, candy counters, tiny storefronts selling glass doodads and fancy-packed CDs. Incense and candles. Small-bore stereo systems. He front-followed, watching her from across the building in hopes that he might seem less obvious. After about ten minutes it dawned on him that she might call the police—the stalking laws being what they were. So he let the tall young woman go and started following another woman, a little older and a little heavier, not as good-looking, with a really pronounced butt. He followed her for a while. She had a boyfriend with her, kind of a goofy-looking guy who looked as if he might have been an engineer. He was awfully clean-cut. He looked at Vaughn a couple of times as if to warn him off, but Vaughn kept following. What was the guy to do? Vaughn was older, *of a certain age,* and was taking a little exercise in the terminal while waiting for a plane. But by then Vaughn had lost interest in the girl and wasn't interested in upsetting the boyfriend.

He went into the hamburger joint at the end of the con-

174

course and ordered a plain burger and a Diet Coke, and he went to the counter to pay for it but didn't have any change. There was an older woman behind the register, a woman about sixty-five with white hair. Her name tag was blank. She seemed nice. She asked him how he was doing, and he said he was doing fine, and he asked her how *she* was doing, and she said she was doing fine, that every day was a better day than the last.

He said, "Pardon me?"

She said, "That's just the way it is. It's the way I look at life, the way things go for me. I could tell you a thing or two. You've got to wait for your burger anyway."

"That's right," he said.

So the woman said, "We've got this hamster. He's a tiny little thing. Kind of a dwarf hamster. We call him Teeny-Weeny. Every morning I get up and I say, 'Good morning, Teeny-Weeny. How are you this morning? Rise and shine!' And then I go about my morning business. I clean myself up, I have a little breakfast, I take care of my husband, Harold—he's close by seventy, soon. Around nine or ten I get ready to come here to work, and I kiss Harold on the forehead, and I stop by the hamster cage and I say, 'I got to go to work now. You be a good boy today, Teeny-Weeny. I'll see you later. I love you, Teeny-Weeny,' and then I come on to work. And I'm just filled with the pleasures, you know?"

Another customer came up and Vaughn stood aside so the other customer could pay his bill, and the woman took his money and made change and told him to have a good day.

"So anyway," she said, gesturing to draw Vaughn back toward her. "I come over here and put in a full day's work, a full shift. I get people food, I talk to them—it just could not be

175

better. At night I go home at the end of my shift, and there's Harold in his chair watching television, and there's Teeny-Weeny in his little cage, and I say, 'Hello Teeny-Weeny, I'm home!' Well, then I go over and let him out of his cage and let him crawl all over me for a while. Sometimes I put him down on Harold and let him crawl on Harold. Sometimes I leave him in his cage. One time we got him a special fire truck that went in his cage, you know?"

"Uh-huh," Vaughn said. "Like a hamster fire truck?"

"That's right. We got him his own fire truck, but he never did like that fire truck because it always turned over on him, and he'd get caught underneath it, and he'd get kind of nervous when that happened. I'd open up the cage and take the truck off him and tell him, 'It's okay. Don't you worry, Momma's right here.' And I'd pet him a little—he liked that. Anyway, after I get home Harold and me will have some dinner, go on and watch some TV, then when it's time to go to bed, I'll holler out from the bedroom, 'Good night, Teeny-Weeny. We love you!' And we'll go on to sleep, don't you know? We've been doing that for some years. And every day is just better than the last."

She turned and looked at the grill. The cook was standing there listening to her, and the burger was burning. "I think your burger's done," she said to Vaughn.

"You're right," the grill guy said. "We're ready."

"You want me to have him cook you another one?" she said.

"No, that one's fine. Just give me that one and my Diet Coke, and I'll be out of your hair."

"You meeting somebody today?" she said.

"I'm meeting my brother. He's coming in from Washington State," Vaughn said.

"Oh, way up there by Alaska, isn't it?" she said.

"That's right," he said.

"I always wanted to go to Alaska," she said. "I'd take Harold and Teeny-Weeny and go up there on one of those boats, you know what I mean? We'd ride along on that big white boat. Boy, that would be the time."

"How old is Teeny-Weeny?" Vaughn said.

"I don't really remember," she said. "He's pretty old, though."

"You take him on trips?" he said.

"We have," she said. "We took him on a trip up the Natchez Trace, all the way to Nashville, Tennessee. That was something. Took Teeny-Weeny and Harold up there. I did all the driving. We did that on our vacation last summer. It was fun. We let Teeny-Weeny out in the car. He ran around. Sometimes he got under the seat—that was a little difficult when he got under the seat. He'd get stuck under there and start squealing, and we'd have to pull off the highway and get Harold out and get in the backseat and reach up under there and get Teeny-Weeny out. He did fine most of the way. Sometimes he sat on the armrest—we'd pull the armrest down and he'd sit up on that for a long time. Trouble was he kept getting stuck. He doesn't like to get stuck much. Fact is, that's probably the last thing he likes—getting stuck under something or having something fall on him. He's got one of those wheels, you know. He likes that pretty well. Makes a racket, though, when I'm trying to sleep."

She was a short woman, very short but well-proportioned.

Her head did not come up above the top of the cash register. He wondered if there was some relation between her physical stature and her affection for the hamster. He wondered about Harold and about their house. He wondered about everything.

He got his change and slid onto the first stool by the register, keeping an eye on the woman, and took a bite out of the burger and a pull on the straw in the Diet Coke. He scanned the place for some pretty women to gaze at while chewing.

When Newton got off the plane he gave Vaughn a magazine he'd been carrying, some West Coast city magazine with a picture of himself on the cover—a feature about his company. After the awkward greetings and the wait at the baggage claim, they went out through a subterranean corridor to the parking garage. Newton looked way too healthy and bigger than Vaughn remembered. He looked a little like their father, but a bigger version of him, pumped up, everything about him bigger, inflated. His father, bloated.

"Glad you could come," Vaughn said, as they emerged from the tunnel. He kept stepping away from his brother to get a better look. Newton looked less big once they got above ground.

"Thanks," Newton said. "Good to get off that plane."

"You look terrific," Vaughn said.

"Yeah. I've been working out for a while, since, you know, Meredith passed. Not much else to do, really."

"Sorry about that," Vaughn said.

Newton flapped a hand. "I've just about rejoined the land

of the living by now," he said. "You've got to let these things play out in their own time."

They got to the car and stowed the luggage, then headed out to Highway 49 to make it down to the coast highway.

"I'm anxious to see what it looks like after Katrina," Newton said.

"Looks just about like it did then," Vaughn said. "Only drier."

"They're not rebuilding?"

"Plan to, but things are dead slow. I don't know why—money mostly, I think. Storm just leveled everything along the waterfront, and everybody wants to put up a high-rise condominium; but prices are ridiculous, and there's insurance and that stuff on both ends. So mostly it's just as it was fifteen months ago."

"That's crazy," Newton said.

"Pretty much," Vaughn said.

They rode down to the beach and turned west heading out to Menge Road, which was one of the few remaining arteries off the beach highway that still connected to Interstate 10. It also went right by Hidden Lake and Gail's house. The beach highway didn't seem to faze Newton, probably because he had no before pictures to compare with the after.

"I have this fantasy about living on a beach," Newton said. "Looks like there's a lot of land for sale here."

"I have this fantasy about taking women captive and having my way with them," Vaughn said. "Especially young women. I take them to this place, to this room, lock the door, do anything I want. I touch them. I comb their hair. I unbutton their clothes. I worry, though—"

"I'd worry if I were you," Newton said. He swung his hand out and popped Vaughn on the shoulder.

"What if they're not wearing pretty underclothes?" Vaughn said.

"That'd be a shame," Newton said. "For a sick puppy like you."

"You shouldn't come in here saying things like that."

"You shouldn't be joking about stealing women," Newton said. "What kind of guy are you? You're old. You should have stopped looking at women years ago."

"Have you?" Vaughn said.

"I'm younger than you are," Newton said. "I'm not that interested, but if I were I could look because I'm still viable. But I'm more interested in women my own age—you know, people with shared experiences, a shared cultural base. The same ideas about the world, something we share."

"I'd just like to share their panties," Vaughn said.

"That's not funny, Vaughn," Newton said.

Vaughn rubbed his forehead a minute, looked at his brother, then looked back at the road. "Just fucking with you, Newton. You know? Jokes are still viable in the Deep South. We do jokes. We think they're funny. We kid around. Know what I mean? We don't have our heads so far up our rears that we can't see a joke coming about a mile away."

"Some jokes are less funny than others," Newton said. "Anyway, Gail was plenty upset when she called. What's the deal with you two?"

"We divorced a year ago. So I'm living with this other woman, and Gail's running around with some high-school kid, a tree-trimmer apparently. So the guy beats her up one night maybe a month ago and what am I going to do? She asked me to stay at the house. We came when called."

"She told me," Newton said.

"So now we're all there, all three of us. The kid, Tony, is around, apparently. He was over the other night, middle of the night, in his truck, in the yard. Yelling. We had a sit-down. He wasn't disgusting, just sort of, like, unreal in the way kids are when they're just getting started as people. And ridiculous, like peanut butter without bread. And has no sense of context, any context."

"Complete with tattoos? Gail said he tattooed her neck," Newton said.

"I didn't see any tattoos. With Gail, he drew his name like a tattoo on her neck. In ballpoint. Like we used to do at St. Anne's. Then he beat the shit out of her."

"She said they had a fight," Newton said.

"Well, he won," Vaughn said. "She went to the hospital."

Newton waved his hand toward the windshield. "Why are you going so slow here?" Cars were whizzing by them in both directions.

"I don't go fast anymore. I used to go fast, and now I don't go fast," Vaughn said. "Since the crash."

"You're a traffic hazard out here. Would you get over to the right if you're going to go this slow?"

"Fine," he said. Vaughn put on the blinker, looked over his shoulder, looked in the rearview mirror, looked in the side mirror, looked in Newton's side mirror, looked in the rearview mirror again, looked over his shoulder again, then eased over into the right lane.

After another minute Newton said, "You did all that for me?"

"Hey! You're catching on. So, how long are you going to be with us?"

"As long as it takes," he said. "Get your blinker."

"Okay," Vaughn said, switching off the turn signal.

They drove along in silence for a few minutes. Vaughn thought his brother was a smug somebody. He wondered how he got to be so smug, so full of himself. You give a guy a couple of breaks and give him a bunch of money, put his face in the newspaper, give him a business. It kind of goes to his head after a while.

"Business good?" Vaughn said.

"Fine," Newton said. "After a while it's just counting money. I wish I had some new project."

Newton had strange facial hair. It was on his chin and under his lip but nowhere else. It was very well kept. The part on his chin looked like a large, well-cared-for mole. Vaughn had a hard time remembering Newton as the kid he'd played with years before. They had done all this stuff together, played soldiers, cowboys, gone to archery classes, played pool and Ping-Pong and gone to school and dated girls and hung out. It was kind of hard to feature that so many decades later.

Vaughn spent the rest of the drive time thinking about what it meant to love your brother—how it might be possible, how it was possible to not like him very much and still recognize him as part of your life and let him into your life in a way that you didn't let anybody else in. Take him for granted. Assume him. Vaughn was sure his life was better when Newton was two or three thousand miles away, and was sure his life was going to be more difficult now that Newton was closer than that.

Newton wanted doughnuts. Didn't they always want doughnuts? First thing? So Vaughn pulled into the Krispy Kreme and got in line. He said, "Gail writes down in a little book the names of people who are going to get murdered, like Mrs. Robert Blake. She keeps a book of tragedies."

"Two chocolate-covered and one custard-filled," Newton said.

They crept up to the squawk box and Vaughn placed the order and the voice of the woman came out of the little box. He had some difficulty, because she thought he was saying mustard when he was saying custard, but eventually she got it. They inched forward behind the Dick Tracy Chrysler that was in front of them.

"So," Newton said. "Things are pretty rough." He was stretching out in the car in some way that seemed unattractive and way too personal. Too much twisting and picking at his clothes.

"They've been that way for a while," Vaughn said.

"Yeah, but rougher now?"

"Did Gail say that?"

"We talk," Newton said. "She calls me. We're friends. We've got some special connections."

"Uh-huh. That's good," Vaughn said. "And you text; you text a lot. Now, me, I don't text too much. I've texted in the past, but not so much now."

"Come on, Vaughn, don't do that," Newton said, sighing, looking out his side window at a Shell station that bordered on the drive-through side of the Krispy Kreme. "That was way back when. I just meant we're friends. So we talk. She's had a hard year."

"She's not alone," Vaughn said.

There was silence in the car for a minute or two, then Newton tried another angle. "You ever think about the parents?"

"All the time," Vaughn said. "Sometimes more than think,

too. Father's pipe tobacco, it's like always turning up. Very peculiar. We didn't do such a good job with Father."

"He didn't deserve a good job," Newton said. "He was a creep."

"Whoa. Big man," Vaughn said. "He took care of you pretty well."

"Not really. I got what I got by working around him. He was kind of a fool, I guess. Mother was pleasant, at least."

"It's a poorer place for their absence," Vaughn said. "Both of them."

Newton turned to look at him. "That's what you think? Really? Not me. Our father was a sick fuck. I wanted to take pictures of him after he died so I could always prove to myself he was dead."

"Everybody says that shit," Vaughn said.

Newton held up his hands as if in surrender. "Well, say hello for me when you're thinking about them. I remember Mother sometimes. She could have made something of herself if she'd wanted to."

"Prick," Vaughn said.

"Fuck off," Newton said.

They were far enough along in the line now that they were next to a window that opened into the back of the Krispy Kreme where the machinery was that the workers used to make the doughnuts. Some kid with a Mohawk and a scraggly goatee was in there yanking dough out of a big pan on top of a pickup-truck-sized machine that turned the dough into doughnuts. The kid looked none too clean.

"So what's going to happen here anyway?" Newton said. "I'm sure you've got this all figured out. Just tell me now so I don't make any mistakes when it comes to my turn."

"I don't know," Vaughn said. "She wants me to come back. I'm not coming back. She's having trouble. She's had trouble with boyfriends, and she has weird ideas about things. She thinks she's psychic or something. Like I said, she said she predicted Robert Blake's wife's death."

"Did she?" Newton said.

"Maybe," Vaughn said. "When did he shoot his wife?"

"Six or seven years ago," Newton said.

"She could have," he said. "She was paying attention then to stuff in those magazines you get at the grocery. Sometimes she reads those."

"Tabloids," he said.

"I guess. *Screen* and *People*—the ones that always have Brad Pitt on the cover."

There was some trouble ahead of them up at the take-out window. The black woman in the Chrysler was arguing with the Krispy Kreme guy. They were shoving a flat box of doughnuts back and forth. Vaughn and Newton sat in line and stared. Voices were raised. Slang was used. Doughnuts flew.

20

Seeing Newton brought back a lot of unpleasant memories. Whatever the truth, Vaughn had counted his brother as their parents' favorite. Parents pretend they love their children equally, care about them equally; but as a child you always know. And don't parents always prefer the youngest? It was unpleasant, but Vaughn knew all children went through it, got used to it eventually, got enough of the affection, the support, the nurture to get by. But he had never quite forgotten.

Newton was a hero in grade school. He was a hero in high school. He was a hero when he went off to college. He was everybody's favorite. He was funny and good-looking. He was charming. Their mother used to hug him endlessly, as if she took every opportunity. Their father liked taking Newton into the den for serious conversations, discussions of politics, religion, morality, and Newton was always ready to do that, always able and willing to do that. He liked discussing things with their father man-to-man. Vaughn would wake up late on the weekend and go by that part of the house, and there they'd be, sitting in the two chairs talking, looking out the window at the backyard, the pristine backyard, talking man-to-man.

Vaughn had a few opportunities, of course, but he was a kid with less to say than his younger brother; he was less forthcoming than Newton, less brilliant, less charming. He was not such a success in school, had fewer friends, and the friends he did have were much less welcome at the house. In fact, Vaughn's friends were mostly losers of one kind or another. And Vaughn was fat as a kid. He wore "Husky" jeans and khakis. His mother had to take him to a special store to get these jeans. And they weren't the right jeans, because the makers of the right jeans wouldn't stoop to making "Husky" jeans. Vaughn was taller, but he had a bad complexion, whereas Newton did not. Vaughn's hair stuck out in spikes that he tried putting hair tonic on to get under control, without much success. Vaughn's hair jiggled when he walked. Newton's hair was smooth and graceful.

So having Newton jet in for the crisis with Gail was not fun. Having Newton stay at the house, set himself up in the fourth bedroom, walk through the place and look at the house Vaughn had bought some years before, appraise it in a way, was not so comfortable. Newton would notice things about the house—the construction, the finishes, the upkeep—that he did not think so well of, and he would mention these things in an offhand, purportedly helpful, but nevertheless demeaning way. And Newton would look at Greta, as if somehow Greta was part of the problem, or as if she didn't measure up.

That first night after Newton arrived, they went to eat at the

Thai restaurant. Vaughn and Gail had been to this restaurant once, years before. It had been wiped out by the hurricane, but was relocated almost immediately in a strip shopping center in the space previously occupied by the Oreck vacuum cleaner store. Vaughn and Greta carefully avoided the Thai restaurant, but Newton wanted Thai, and Gail had told him there was a wonderfully authentic little Thai place in town, so they ended up there. In their section of the coast a lot of college kids and some of the professors ate the food there, which was one reason Vaughn disliked the place. Another was that there were always ants in a trail along the wainscoting. The lighting was too bright, the food was soggy and stained and badly presented, and the place itself was in sore need of attention. It was altogether discouraging, like eating in an Oreck store in a desolate strip shopping center.

Newton and Gail pored over the menu and Gail gave him detailed descriptions of each dish. She let on that she and Tony often used the Thai restaurant as a rendezvous. "I figured Vaughn wouldn't look for us here," she said.

They were sitting at a yellow linoleum-topped table with almost-matching chairs covered in yellow plastic. They were in the middle of the small aisle between two rows of booths. Along the wainscot next to the booths on the west wall, the parade of ants was in full flower, running from the back of the restaurant toward the front. Vaughn elbowed Greta and raised his head in the direction of the ant line. She glanced and made a face to tell him to shut up. When it was her turn to order, she said, "Why don't you order for me, Gail? I haven't eaten much Thai."

Whereupon Gail and Newton discussed at some length what Greta might and might not like.

"Maybe I should have something not so good," Greta said.

Vaughn ordered noodles and the cow pea salad, a dish he'd read about in a newspaper article years before. The four of them were way too close together at this table. The table was small. There was barely enough room for a napkin dispenser and a little flower. They hunched around this little table prepared for conversation as they waited for their food, but the conversation was slow in coming. It mostly fell to Gail and Newton to catch up. She asked a lot of questions about his business, his late wife, his life in the Great Northwest. Newton was lonely, but he was fond of where he lived and felt fortunate to have moved there before it was popular and sought after.

About his business he said, "Oh, there's hardly anything left to do. We did so well with the company that I'm pretty much out of the loop now. I have a few small projects, but other than that, I'm afraid I don't do much."

He seemed strangely overstuffed. His shirt was too small, his trousers, too. Both were wrinkled, but he was not a grunge guy, he was a tucked-in guy, so the wrinkles gave the impression of being well-planned. His shirt was madras. Strange, Vaughn thought. He hadn't seen a madras shirt in some time, though he was aware madras had made it back into style a few years before. Gail had told him.

As he sat across the table from Newton, what he was thinking was: Maybe he'll just explode right here.

It wasn't that he was fat, but he was burly. Like he'd gained a lot of weight and it hadn't settled in his stomach or his backside. It was all-over weight. It was in his arms, ankles, thighs, cheeks, temples, neck, and shoulders. It was as if he had taken Newton from ten years ago and made a second skin an inch or so thick and carefully sewn it on him, in the style of that guy in the movie. He was a Hefty bag, Vaughn's brother.

"So what's all this stuff you guys are going through down here?" Newton said. "Vaughn's been filling me in, but it sounds crazy."

"It is a little crazy," Gail said.

"Nothing much," Vaughn said. "There was some messy business with this guy and she asked us to move over, and we came over," he said. "Like I told you."

"He's talking about Tony," Gail said.

"Right. Gail's been dating him, and he got a little out of hand," Vaughn said. "Like I told you, he was at the house the other night. He's not exactly covered in contrition, but he wasn't unbearable."

"That's news," Gail said. "You liked him?"

"I didn't mind him," he said. "He came in and we talked. He wasn't that bad, I mean, apart from, you know—"

"Amazing," she said.

"Anyway, things are getting back on track."

"He's leaving out a lot," Gail said.

"I am leaving out a lot," Vaughn said. "I thought Newton might appreciate that."

"Don't start," Gail said.

"We don't need to involve Newton in our problems, Gail," Vaughn said.

"That's why he's here," she said.

"That's why I'm here," Newton said.

At this point Greta sort of touched Vaughn's arm in a way that he liked a lot. She touched his forearm on the table, sort of patted it—just once or twice. She turned and said to Newton, "Why *are* you here? I know I'm not family, but I don't quite get it."

"Gail and I go way back," Newton said.

"I've heard that," Greta said.

"We had a sort of friendship," Newton said.

"And that's why you're here to help out with Gail and Vaughn?" Greta said.

"And Tony. And you," Newton said.

"And me?" Greta said. "Huh. Feature that. I made the team."

That produced nervous strain, visible on two of the four faces. Then food arrived, so trouble was sidestepped. The food was stringy and peculiar, and Gail and Newton loved it. Vaughn put some of his on Greta's plate while no one was watching. Greta put the food back on his plate while everyone was watching. Gail waved at them as if they were children. She and Newton carried on a conversation about his life in the Great Northwest and their life together before she and Vaughn met. There wasn't much of a story there. Vaughn didn't think their relationship, or his subsequent marriage to Gail, seemed too odd at the time, though now it seemed odder. Gail and Newton were better suited for each other than he and Gail. By the time Katrina hit, his marriage had long since looked like a basket of maladies. They'd had good times in the early going, but recent years were something less than satisfying—too much distance, too many differences. And when his life felt that way he always wondered about other people—in the stores, in their very clean cars, walking together in their heavily-starched clothing: Were they content with each other, or was the only contentedness they'd ever had what they'd had in their first years together?

191

Thinking of that, he regarded Newton, who was a widower and who had been living alone for a couple of years, and his own ex-wife, Gail, who seemed very interested in her conversation with his brother. They probably had searing and wonderful memories of that month they were together so many years ago. And so, as Vaughn thought about it there at the Thai joint, which was called Yum Yum, it suddenly didn't seem altogether odd that Newton would come thousands of miles across the country to Gail's rescue now, so many years later. For the first time recognizing the possible virtues of Newton's visit, Vaughn fetched up his chopsticks and started to enjoy himself, pursuing his noodles with a fierce new vigor. He smiled and nodded when others looked his way. He made little noises of appreciation, pointing at the food. He reached for Greta's hand and gave it a resolute squeeze.

21

Three days later on Saturday morning Vaughn woke up to find Gail at the door of his room, knocking discreetly. She was dressed and made up and on her way out to the store or something. She looked nervous and fidgeted with her fingers.

"How are you?" she said, peeking in the room to see if Greta was there. She wasn't, as it happened.

"I'm kind of sleepy," he said. "Time is it?"

"Almost nine," she said. "Listen, uh, I wanted to thank you for everything, for all these years, and for this thing, coming over here and all that. It really is kind of you to interrupt everything and move in and look after me."

"Sure," he said. "My pleasure. Are you—"

"Going away," Gail said. "I'm going with Newton out to his place, just for a kind of a look-see, you know? I mean, the way he talks about it sounds so great, and he wants to go back, so I thought I'd go with."

"Oh," Vaughn said.

"I'm just taking a break from everything," she said. "Clearing the air, standing back, taking a look at the big picture, that kind of thing."

"Big picture," he said. "How about Tony?"

She looked positively adolescent, twisting herself around there in the hallway. "Well, you know, I don't care that much about Tony, really, all things considered. I didn't see him as a long-termer."

Vaughn nodded. He was sleepy and his hair was dervished up and he just kept nodding at her. He said, "Okay. When are you coming back?"

"I don't know. Could be right away, could be longer—we haven't decided. I'm just playing things by ear. I always wanted to see the Great Northwest."

Then she was backing away down the hall. She said, "You guys should stay here if you want. Keep the place warm. Not a problem. Invite Eddie if you want. We're just about packed. We'll be pulling out any minute."

"It's short notice, isn't it?" he said.

She turned and grinned. "Yeah, I guess so. You don't mind, do you?"

Well, he did mind. But then again, this was Gail, mercurial Gail. She was able to move in a big hurry. Gail had called Newton, after all. Maybe Vaughn wasn't the first to imagine the possibilities.

"I don't like him," Greta said, when he got her up and they went downstairs to wave good-bye as Newton and Gail headed out of the driveway. "I didn't like him the minute I laid eyes on him."

"He's fine," he said. "Wave."

"He's a snot-nosed somebody," she said, waving at the car. "He's real proud of himself. Far prouder than he need be."

"He's done very well," he said.

"He's a snot," she said.

"He came all the way down here to get Gail," Vaughn said.

"I know that," Greta said. "So gallant. Couldn't she have sort of flown up there on her own? You don't care about her going off with him now?"

"It's odd," Vaughn said. "It's very odd. But it's a load off. At least for the moment."

"That's what you think of her—a load?"

"Quit it," he said. "I love her, but you've been around her awhile, what do *you* think?"

"I think she's a load, but that's me. I never was in love with her."

"No, you got it right," he said. "I don't imagine it's over, though."

"She's going to call and e-mail and have other problems and she's going to need to talk to you about them," she said.

"Right," he said.

"And she's going to get together with Newton, and they're going to live together. Something like that?" she said.

"Could be. Kind of looked that way, didn't it?"

"Looked like they were made for each other," Greta said.

"I thought the same thing," he said.

———

The beach west of Waveland was never developed, not before the hurricane, and not after. The land out there was marshy and mostly unused. One night about a week after Gail left, Vaughn and Greta drove out that way and found an abandoned beach house up on creosoted twelve-by-twelve wood pilings across the highway from the water. There wasn't another building for half a mile toward town, and west there wasn't anything at all except a shrimp-packing house that had been swamped by Katrina and the remnants of a casino that had failed out there where the highway dead-ended. They got out the flashlight and went up the stairs, sat on the deck of this beach house, which was a little delicate, being as most of the deck was gone and what was left was rotting and dotted with holes you could fall through. The rest of the place was equally torn up. There wasn't much of a roof, no glass, the doors were gone, and it didn't smell so good. They were outside, sitting with their backs to the front wall, watching the moon rise in the east. Small boats passed going east to west. Fishing, Vaughn presumed, running with as few lights as possible. Along the horizon in the distance there were gold lights on oil rigs. The sky was lit up with stars.

He pointed and said, "If you don't look at them you can see them flash."

"That's what they're there for," Greta said. "They're stars."

"Amen," he said.

"So, like, to summarize," she said, "you failed your family—your mother and father and your brother—and now you've failed your wife. Your brother had to come in and successfully sweep her away, and so you've failed again. Is that about the size of it—you're sort of a failure birth to death? A cry in the darkness kind of thing?"

"Not exactly a cry," he said.

"A whimper?" she said. "A foul noise?"

"Something," he said. "You've got something there."

They didn't say anything for a few minutes and felt the breeze as it climbed over them. The moon was streaking up the water.

"You know what I think about your father? I think he loved you. I think he probably did the best he could, and he was probably hurt in the end, but I think he never stopped loving you. If he knew you at all."

"I don't know. How would you know that, anyway?"

"You listen," she said. "When people talk. And you read what they're saying, and you back out all their opinions, you try to figure what they're angry about, and worried about, and you add or subtract that from the picture they're giving you, and then you maybe get another picture from somebody else, and you paste that in, and then you get a report from somebody else about the person you got the first picture from, and that changes things a little, and after a while you get a pretty good idea about the person everybody else is talking about."

"Huh," Vaughn said.

"He forgives you," she said. "That's what I get. He loved you and he wanted to be better than he was."

"He would forgive," Vaughn said. "That was him all over."

Each day after Gail's sudden departure with his brother, Vaughn felt a little better, a little cleaner, a little more relieved and comfortable. He was still surprised, too, but mostly he felt unlatched from a responsibility that he hadn't really wanted in the first place. Some kind of ease had settled on him and replaced everything that had been getting at him since the night of his birthday dinner at the Palomino Restaurant or maybe before that, maybe even since the divorce. Maybe even be-fore *that*. When you live with a woman for a long time, after a while you make a lot of excuses for what you don't feel, but unless you're a fool you don't believe the woman is at fault. It's that the world changes beneath your feet. Things go slow at first and the change is so small that it's almost impercep-tible, and you pay it no mind. And then later, years later, the change seems huge and it seems to have occurred overnight. Suddenly you aren't the person you were. And then, where once you thought not wanting what you used to want was punishment, suddenly you think it may be a blessing.

And things stand still.

You watch the moon reflected on the swarming gulf water, and you think, That's enough. That's all I want. I just want to sit on this broken-down deck on this night in this cool weather with this breeze blowing over me and watch this moon lift into the sky—remarkably oval, remarkably pearly, remark-ably aloft. And you want to think this in just these words, and you know the words aren't right, they aren't even close, and that doesn't matter. The deal is that it's just the moon in the sky reflected on the gulf, the water hissing and receding, and you're in the middle of it, and you're just a small part, an un-important part, but a part nonetheless. Your job is to be there so the moon can hit something when it shines at the earth. You are something to hit. And that's the way it is for the rest of the world, too. What people say and what they think, who they are, what they think about you, what they ask of you, what you want, what you give them does not matter. It's that way for everything—the sounds of the night, the breeze on the back of your hand, on your knee, the shoe hanging off your foot, the pressure of the plastic chair against your elbow or your forearm, the sound of the light waves falling on the beach, the twinkle of the lights on the oil platforms offshore, the smells, and all the stars in the sky, the shadows that crawl past—you're something to hit. You're a receiver. You're an antenna.

Vaughn said something about this to Greta, who nodded and threw something that she'd been playing with off the deck—maybe it was a chip of wood she'd picked up, he didn't know; but he saw her throw it and admired the motion of her arm, a remarkably wooden motion, as if her arm was not connected to her body in any way, as if her arm, peculiarly white and almost translucent in the decaying moonlight, had a mind of its own.

22

Vaughn and Greta spent the next few weeks on the deck at the hijacked beach house, shuttling back and forth between the beach house and her house on Mary Magdalene and Gail's house. They were at sixes and sevens. They ate a lot of Chinese food. They ate barbecued ribs, pulled pork, Key lime pie. They ate steamed gyoza. They ate hamburgers in cars in parking lots and French fries and onion rings and chocolate shakes. They ate fried oysters, calamari, redfish, flounder, and pine nuts. They spoke softly.

They'd spent a lot of time on Gail, taken her on as a project, a community project—something they might figure out, even repair—and it wasn't entirely fair, insofar as Gail wasn't exactly clued in on the deal. But now that Gail had departed they were free to do whatever without worrying too much about her, who she was talking to, who she was meeting in the middle of the night, where she might be sitting in her car at dawn scribbling notes to her friends on the backs of business cards. Now, in hindsight, Vaughn wondered if moving over there had been foolhardy. Ex-spouses were never quite ex enough, and weeks, months, years later they were still close by, attached to your world. You had to pay attention to them. And in this case there was the more immediate need: protection. Tony was around. He had beaten her silly, and maybe it wouldn't happen again if they were at the house with her. In fact, it hadn't happened again, but Tony was still very much in the picture throughout, even if he and Gail saw each other only on the sly, as if Greta and Vaughn were the parents and Gail the bad-girl daughter, sneaking out late at night to meet up with her too-rough friends.

So when Gail pulled out, Greta and Vaughn didn't know quite what to do. They sat out by the sea night after night watching the flounder fishermen, watching the moon, listening to the sound of the surf, leaning their backs against the tattered walls of somebody's given-up beach house, a house torn apart in the storm a year before, but also in who knows how many previous storms, and now, finally, recognized as more trouble than it was worth.

On one night when the sky was just speckled with stars, a thin haze around the perimeter, the half moon rising in the east with its reflection trailing toward them over the surf, moving sidewinder style, like a bright snake moving across a dark desert floor, Greta asked him what they were going to do, and he said he did not know. He said he hadn't the slightest idea. He said, "Why don't we just do what we used to do?"

"What's that?" she said.

"I don't remember," he said. "Go to dinner, watch television. Remember that big-screen television we used to watch all the time over at your house?"

"Eddie's watching that one now," she said.

"Maybe we can get another one," he said. "We could stay at Gail's house and move the TV, put it at the foot of the bed, and get into bed every night and watch it. We could watch all the tripe they serve up, the cop shows, the *CSI* shows, Court TV, all that cable stuff like National Geographic's *Explorer* and *Extreme Machines,* and reality cop shows like that one from the files of Dayle Hinman, and we could watch news and sports and those incredible game shows and *Lost,* which seems to have a lot of sex in it, and HGTV, all those house-buying shows, and design shows, and stupid reality shows, all the gory excess of this stupid and vulgar culture, the idiot news every night, with a blown-up building one night and a mother killing her children the next, and with women disappearing off the streets and guys who sit in the Wal-Mart parking lot the better to watch the women, and guys who will tell you that and do it, too, and the cooking shows, the British TV shows, the high-definition shows, the HBO specials, and the sex shows. We could do that every night, and while away the hours."

"Uh, no," Greta said.

The surf that night was a sort of silvery green, a green that was barely perceptible as green but which was nevertheless green. They watched the lighted fishing boats slide across the water, listened to the groan of trees pushed by wind, caught out of the corners of their eyes the giant birds that flew inland every once in a while, dark shadows against a lighter sky. Pelicans, maybe, off schedule. Sea birds.

"Is she coming back?" Greta asked.

"Don't know," he said. "But if she is, we don't have to do what we've already done. If she comes back she's on her own."

"Until the first time somebody beats her up. Or when she calls with some crisis, or when she says she loves you and wants you back. Then what?"

"I'm going to hide behind you," Vaughn said. "I'm going to be direct and honest and forthright."

"So you're quitting her? For real?"

"You're all about the movies, huh?" Vaughn said.

"I don't buy it," Greta said.

"Wait and see."

"We should bring peanut butter sandwiches," she said. "To-morrow. Are we coming tomorrow? Let's bring peanut butter sandwiches. Do you want to make them or should I?"

"Does it have to be decided right this minute?" he said.

A motorboat with a red light on the front of it and a white light at the rear, lights the size of Christmas lights, trolled across their vision left to right. The lights reflected in the surf, the sound of the motor constant—a drone, an ache, like a door opening, opening, opening, like someone saying *Ahh* endlessly.

"What about money?" Greta said.

"We have money," he said. "If we don't move fast or travel to distant lands, we'll be fine. We'll live the small life."

"Hmm," Greta said, as if considering the virtues of this. "*La petite vie.*"

The boat with the lights came across again, going in the other direction now, now shining a spotlight up on the house where they were sitting, shining the light right in their eyes, heading toward them and then crossing in front of them, very close to the beach.

"I should feel something about Gail," he said. "Or think something. But I don't. Nothing. She's like a neighbor now."

"Wow. You are the quick and the mean," Greta said.

"Not," he said.

"Is that the way it is with you about everything? When you're done, you're done? I'm beginning to get the idea that you really have checked out."

"Something like that," he said. "I don't think I have to be heard on every single subject. When I was a younger man . . ."

"And you were a younger man only weeks ago."

"Here's the new me: a nice, easygoing, regular guy. If somebody does something stupid, it's fine with me. If somebody on TV does something stupid, it's fine with me. If somebody on TV does something stupid and gets paid millions of dollars, also fine."

"You're out of this world," Greta said. "You're a go-along guy."

"Finally," he said.

"You're following your bliss."

"Well, not exactly," he said. "If we're getting uglier and coarser, as my father said, who wants to live in a toilet? Is there a point at which it stops getting coarser and starts getting finer? Is that point coming along, or are we going to miss it? Where's Dad? I want to ask him. If my parents were less coarse, and I am more coarse, maybe my children will complete the cycle and become less coarse."

"Your children?" she said, handing him a brand new bottle of OFF!

"Figuratively," he said. He turned his flashlight on the anti-mosquito can and read the label. " *'Repels mosquitoes that may carry West Nile Virus.'* You picked a good one here."

"You're a coarse piece of business, aren't you?" she said.

Her cell phone rang. It was Eddie calling from the house. He wanted to know if they were coming there later or if they were going to the big house. She looked at Vaughn, asked, and he said, "I don't know. Whatever you want to do is fine."

"Why?" she said into the telephone, then listened. "That's fine," she said. "We'll see you tomorrow. Right." Then she closed the phone, slipped it back into her shirt pocket. "He has a friend."

"Oh, my god," he said. "Of what denomination?"

"He did not say," she said.

"Should we move him back to the garage? It would be mean to move him to the garage," he said.

"If we move over there, he's going back," she said. "But for the moment I'm enjoying this brief respite from responsibility delivered to us by the departure of your ex-wife, the lovely Gail, the brotherfucker."

"Okay, that's over the line. There's a line there and you're over it."

"Couldn't resist," she said.

23

Three weeks to the day after she left, Gail called to say she and Newton were having trouble. "We're not getting along," she said. "He doesn't really want me here. He says he loves me, but he's not in love with me. He says he needs to find himself. He says he's a work in progress and he's just been reading about this, and understanding this, and getting back with me after all this time is not the way forward for him, at least not yet."

"Well, that surprises me," Vaughn said.

"Are you being wry?"

"I thought I was," he said.

"Are you trying to hurt me?"

"No, I'm not. I've never tried to hurt you. Not once."

"That's true. I remember that about you," she said.

There was a silence on the phone. He toyed with some

shells that Greta had picked up on the beach on their travels to the beach house.

Gail said, "Vaughn? Are you there? Vaughny?"

"I'm here. I'm here. What?" he said.

"I may have to come back there," she said.

"There are worse things," he said.

"We're not getting back together, are we?" she said.

"I don't think so," he said.

"This is like really the end of our marriage," she said.

"I think so. Yes," he said.

"It's about time, isn't it?" she said.

That caught him. He wasn't ready for that. It didn't seem like something Gail would say. He didn't think it was intended to be mean, but it sounded a little mean. Maybe it was just fatigue. Maybe she was as fatigued as he was.

"I guess it is. We had a good run."

"What's that? Something from some TV movie?" she said.

"Sorry," he said. "But still, it's true. We did have a pretty good run."

There was more silence, and then she said, "Yeah, I guess you're right. It could have lasted two years and been in the dumper."

"What are you going to do when you get back here?" he said.

"*If* I come back," she said. "I don't know. Same shit. I may stay here. Maybe I could lean on Newton for a while."

"I thought he loved you but wasn't in love with you?"

"I don't need him to be in love with me," she said. "I need him to like me and to go to dinner with me and to be a close friend occasionally."

"A close friend I don't want to hear about."

"I just need somebody to hang out with," she said. "Hang out is what I do these days. That's what I miss about our marriage. You know, all the time we spent together, messing around, doing nothing. Going to the grocery store."

"Yeah, I know," he said.

"But you've got Greta now," Gail said. "She's a nice woman, Greta."

"If you like the type," he said.

"Come on," Gail said.

"Was a joke," he said.

"Yeah, I completely missed it, you know," Gail said. "I unlearned everything in the last fifteen minutes."

"It was sort of a joke," he said.

"Are you alluding to the fact that, how shall I say, she's rough-hewn?" Gail said.

"I was not alluding to that," he said. "And furthermore, and for the record, she is not rough-hewn, whatever you might mean by that."

"I apologize for that," Gail said.

"Accepted," he said.

When he told Greta that Gail might come back to town, Greta shrugged and shook her head and rolled her eyes and wagged her hands in the air. All at once.

"She gives me the heebie-jeebies," Greta said.

"I don't think she's going to bother us anymore," he said. "We'll probably have to move out of the house."

"I'm ready to go," she said. "Why don't we go tonight?"

"We've got to get Eddie out of your house first," he said.

"I'll call him," Greta said.

So at two o'clock in the morning, they started packing the cars, collecting the stuff they'd brought over from Greta's house, and the stuff they'd accumulated since living at Gail's, slapping it into their two cars. Trip after trip into the big house.

"This is fun," Greta said, passing him on her way in as he was coming out.

"Is it?" he said. He was carrying a bunch of shirts on hangers and a couple of pairs of shoes. She was going back for another load.

"Think this'll work?" Greta said.

"Yes," he said.

"I look forward to it," she said. She gave him a little kiss on the forehead, then pushed him toward the stairs.

It took them only about an hour and a half to pack. They became less careful as the packing went on. At first they maintained a coherent plan, isolating things that didn't want to be folded or didn't want to be crushed or that wanted to be hanging on the rod, which was running across the backseat of her car; but after a while, they were just throwing stuff into both of the cars. It didn't matter. Boxes of cereal landed on top of freshly washed jeans. Skirts were wadded up and stuffed into the space behind the backseat. It was a mess. It was an escape. It was cowboys and Indians.

Closing on four o'clock they trailed through town the few blocks to the beach road, then up to Interstate 10 and across to the Bay St. Louis exit, and down to Greta's place in Waveland. Greta in front in her car, him in his car behind. There was something of the celebration about the trip—the slow drive with the windows down, the clammy gulf air blowing through the car windows, the empty streets, the almost slow-motion of a parade.

He wondered if she was driving so slowly because she was enjoying it or if she had some other motive. Maybe she was showing him something. Sometimes people liked to tell you things without telling you things, he thought. Sometimes they liked to show you things, demonstrate things, and why shouldn't they? Sometimes the things you learned from demonstration stuck with a fierceness that could not be matched.

When they got to Greta's house, Eddie was on the porch, sitting in an aluminum deck chair, drinking a Bud. Monkey was by his side, asleep, upside down. "It's all yours," Eddie said. "I've just been keeping watch. The place is clean as a whistle. You could eat off the floors in there." He wiggled the neck of the beer bottle toward the front door.

He didn't get up to help them unload the cars. They put one of the cars in the driveway and the other in the yard, and then they carried everything inside. Greta's house looked just as it had before they left. Eddie had returned everything to its prior state, as if he had photographed it the morning they left and used the photographs to set things back in order. An episode of Dominick Dunne's Court TV show was running—a story about a fat white guy and his wife, who had fallen in love with a black man and had decided to shoot her husband so that she could be with her new lover. Vaughn couldn't figure out how that qualified for the rich and famous murder show that Dominick Dunne presented, but there it was. They watched it in bits and pieces as they unloaded the cars. Eddie stayed on the porch, nodding every time Vaughn walked past.

"You guys here to stay awhile?" he said on one trip. "I don't mind moving back to the garage apartment," he said on another trip. "You look good totin' that bale," he said on a third trip.

Vaughn said, "You missed me, huh?"

"Is it evident?" Eddie said.

They put all of Greta's stuff in her room and all of Vaughn's stuff in his room, and neither he nor she made any effort to put the stuff away. It was more or less dump-it-on-the-bed time.

After they got everything inside, they got beers and sat outside with Eddie. They were a couple of blocks off the Gulf, but you could still hear the surf, a murmur in the background, and the buzz of a few streetlights, and a few air conditioners cutting on and off around them.

"So, what happened?" Eddie said. "Why this sudden change of heart?"

"Gail's coming back," Vaughn said. "She's probably coming back. Well, I don't know that she's coming back, but she may be coming back."

"We thought we would just get out of the way," Greta said. "Whether she comes back or not."

"I get it," Eddie said.

"Knew you would," she said.

"So, what happens next?" Eddie said.

"What happens next is we're going to bed before the sun comes up."

"Together?" Eddie said.

"We're going to rest awhile," Greta said, patting his arm to tell him she appreciated the joke.

"Then we'll do whatever comes after that," Vaughn said. "When the time rolls around. We're going to try not to worry too much. We're going to take it easy." He looked at Greta, raised his hands, as if to ask her if that was what they were going to do.

She said, "Exactly right."

"We decided we were too involved with my ex-wife," Vaughn said. "I was too involved with my ex-wife. I love my ex-wife, but I'm not in love with my ex-wife. Wait, that can't be right. That's what my brother said."

"You ought to treat your brother better," Eddie said. "I know some guys who never had a brother. I know some guys who had brothers, but they got killed. I know some guys who killed their brothers. That ain't right. It's not what you're supposed to do. I don't know what's wrong with you not getting along with your brother any better than you do. He's your flesh and blood. He's your fruit of the loin, whatever. You should be kind to him and care for him, and he should do the same for you. I don't know what's wrong with the two of you. You make me ashamed to be a person."

"They have a vexed relationship," Greta said. "They're like Siamese fighting fish."

"We're pretty, all right," Vaughn said.

"That's not the part I mean," she said.

"I know all about Siamese fighting fish," Eddie said. "Would you shut the fuck up about Siamese fighting fish? I'm saying this thing with his brother is wrong."

"There's a backstory," Vaughn said. "I have this brother and, you know, everybody liked him."

"Liked him better than you," Eddie said. "He was smarter and prettier. And nicer and funnier and more genuine and less defensive."

"Had more friends," Vaughn said.

"I was listing things people like," Eddie said. "I know some shit. I've been around places. I've met some people. He came up in a different time."

"No, same time," he said.

"He was a smoker," Greta said. "That'll get you some friends right there."

Vaughn looked at her and shook his head. He had no fucking idea. "I think it's getting late," he said. "People are saying stuff."

"It's a fact," she said.

"You should make up with him," Eddie said. "You should get back together with him and make up."

"We're fine," he said. "We've always been just a little bit, you know, edgy with each other."

"He thinks Vaughn's dumb and Vaughn thinks he's dumb, and that's the way that works," Greta said.

"He's not dumb," Vaughn said.

"Well, whatever you want to call it," she said. She stood up and poured the last bit of her beer into the flower bed. "I really don't believe he came down here and took Gail with him back up there to wherever the fuck he went. I really don't get it. I watched it all go on, and I don't believe any of it. I couldn't figure it out."

"I think she likes him better than she likes me," he said.

"She married you," Greta said.

"I know, but he was already gone by then," he said. "They'd had their deal."

213

"When he left here," she said, "when she went with him, did you actually think they were going to stay together up there?"

"No," he said. "Well, I guess I thought it was possible."

There were sirens off in the distance. They were quiet listening to the sirens for a few minutes. The sound was coming toward them, then went past them. The reflected lights shot through the trees on Mary Magdalene Street. Some guy in a milk truck went by. Vaughn pointed to the truck and looked at Greta and said, "Is that a milk truck? They still deliver milk around here?"

"They're keeping up the old ways," she said.

"Why don't we get on the route?" he said. "We could get some milk, have them put it right here on the step."

"You don't like milk, and besides, you can't have milk. I don't like milk. And he doesn't have the right kind of milk anyway."

"You guys want to go see the fire?" Eddie said.

The next day Vaughn called Molly Maids and arranged for them to clean the house on Tilted Tree. He told them where the key was, told the woman on the phone that they should give it their best shot, price was no object he said.

"You want us to blow the place out?" she said. "I'll get one of my teams on it and we'll bust the place down to the paint. That what you want? It's expensive."

"Ground zero," he said. "I want that place spick'n'span," he said. "I want it to look as though nobody ever lived there. I want it to smell like a high mountain pass. I want it too good to be true."

"Gotcha," the woman said.

He spent some time reflecting on Newton, and he guessed he saw the error of his ways. They were family and that meant something—or it might mean something, or in some cases, under the right circumstances, if push came to shove, and with a little luck—well, theoretically that counted. He figured Newton would go on with his life in the Great Northwest, and he would go on with his life in the slums of the South, and from time to time they would talk on the telephone or exchange e-mail messages, but that finally they would remain at a certain distance and that was okay because Newton would never quite get Vaughn and Vaughn would never quite get Newton. Gradually, they would fade back into the backgrounds of each other's lives. They would become wallpaper, set decoration. His life would be Greta and Eddie and whoever else they might take into their little set.

And Newton would always be out there.

It struck Vaughn as odd that a person he'd known so long, who had been central to him for a lifetime, who had been there almost from the crib, became as an adult so far away, so inessential. It was as if Newton had become a member of some other family, like some guy he'd known in high school, or a kid from college, or a designer he'd worked with in an architectural office somewhere. It was odd that once their parents were dead, the rest of the family collapsed of its own weight. He figured it wasn't what was expected, or even what happened all that often. But it seemed to have happened to him, and Greta, too, from the look of things, and Eddie, though he wasn't sure about Eddie because people often had connections their friends never knew of or understood. He wondered if it wouldn't be a better idea to work harder to make a friend out of his brother, to let the difficulties between them slip away, to overlook the parts of Newton's behavior he didn't like and try harder to find the things they shared.

If you were lucky in the world you built yourself a new life as an adult, complete with friends, lovers, partners, rivals, enemies. You replaced the old people with new people, and your party moved along effortlessly, dancing toward death. If you were unlucky you were left to float on the great angry ocean, never to hear the sound of wood hitting wood in the middle of the night in the darkness of the sea. Something like that.

24

Monkey got hit by a car and lost a leg. That was a stinking day. They had him at the vet for almost a week, and when he came home he could barely walk. But that didn't last so long, and after another week he was back at it with a vengeance. Vaughn spent hours practice-walking with him, and at night Monkey snuggled on the couch between them. They tried to console themselves with talk about his having had a good life before the accident, but there was no consolation to be had. "He's just another three-legged dog in a line of three-legged dogs stretching back to the Middle Ages," Greta said.

"I like him better with three legs," Eddie said. "We oughta get a sculpture of the fourth leg or something. Put it in the yard."

"We can sure do that," Vaughn said.

"I hate it," Greta said. "I hate cars and people and shit-all."

Gail called from time to time, and after a while she asked Vaughn to sell the house on Tilted Tree Lane, so he contacted a real estate woman and set that in motion, and the house sold quickly, which was a surprise to all of them. Gail had some people from Biloxi come and pack up her things and put them in storage. The sale price was good and closing went smoothly; and when all was said and done, he sent Gail her half of the proceeds in the form of a bank check.

"You know what you're doing yet?" he asked Gail in a telephone call one night.

"Not yet," she said. "Things are in flux here. Things are changing."

That was all. No further explanation.

"Well," he said, "say hello to Teeny-Weeny for me."

"What?" she said.

"Nothing," he said.

Vaughn and Greta settled into a routine. They stayed home a lot and watched television, ate take-out food, sometimes they played board games with Eddie, when he had nothing better to do, which seemed to be most of the time. The winter came and went, the second since Katrina, and they were fine. Their life was small but not unpleasant.

With his half of the house money, he bought the abandoned beach house where they had spent so much time squatting in the late fall. Fixing it up was a project, but he didn't mind. Greta was a good hand with a hammer, so the renovation went quickly. Before long it was livable. They moved out there, inviting Eddie to move back into the house on Mary Magdalene. This time he insisted on paying rent. He'd gotten

218

a job in town with the Veterans Administration—counseling kids coming back from the war. Vaughn thought he'd taken some night courses when they weren't looking and gotten some kind of degree. He had straightened up and he was flying right, and only after he'd had a couple of beers would he lay into the president, the government, the army, or anybody else who'd ever cost him anything.

Greta had a drafting table in the second bedroom out at the beach house and did all of her design work there. Vaughn helped out now and then, but mostly he worked on the house doing small jobs at a snail's pace. They gave up watching TV after a time. They got satellite radio and liked that—lots of different things to listen to—but pretty soon that stayed off most days as well. They worried about hurricanes, but the place was sturdy and they'd been able to get insurance, though the price was robbery. From a great distance they watched the tedious reconstruction of the Gulf Coast, which, eighteen months after Katrina, was still more or less untouched. The bridge across the bay finally got fixed. Land prices were through the roof and the only development going on was condo stuff, places in Biloxi for sale at six hundred fifty thousand to a million five, it said in the paper. Selling like hotcakes, it said. Vaughn thought he might go crazy being cut off out at the end of the world west of Waveland, being mostly out of touch, not working, not seeing anyone. He once thought everything depended on being in touch; but now, being of a certain age, he was comfortable not knowing much about what was going on in town, or, for that matter, in the state, or the country; though often they watched the news on television, and sometimes he'd read a story or two from the *New York Times* online. He felt guilty about falling away from things, but there was also something about falling away that he found enriching, sort of like clueing him into something that felt like a bigger picture.

He and Greta shared their opinions about what they saw on television—the war, the government, the politicians, the way things were around the country, the tragedies featured on the news all the time, the bewildering atrocities, the stolen women and kidnapped children, the deadly fires, the mutilations, molestations, violations, cruelties, and car chases, the disasters of every kind, the malfeasances and misconduct, the men killing wives and wives killing each other, whatever came up night after night—but their views didn't go much beyond the kitchen table. He had trouble remembering the point of having all those opinions. What were they worth? What did they matter?

Some old dog came up to the deck one day and they petted him. He seemed to want to stay on, so they let him. He slept out on the deck for a while and then they brought him into the house and cleaned him up, gave him a name. They called him Fuzzy, because he was. He was some kind of mutt that looked kind of like one of those Australian cattle dogs—gray with black splotches all over him. He was smart, too. He had a sharp nose and good eyes. He watched everything Monkey did carefully, as if he were doing some kind of leg trick. He fit right in.

Spring was early as usual and they decided to paint the house. Greta wanted to use yellow ochre with white trim and Vaughn thought the house ought to be a strong burnt orange. They flipped on it and he won. So that's the way they went. There weren't any other beach houses out there—they were way to the west, pretty far out from the town, about where they wanted to be. For a while Eddie came out all the time, but he got tired of that. Maybe they weren't interesting enough. He stopped showing up for dinners and they never saw him. Finally he came out and said he'd bought a piece of land in Pearlington, a tiny town halfway to Slidell, and he was moving over there. His work was taking him into New Orleans a few times a week, he said. There was still a lot of trouble there, and he figured he could help out.

So they put the house on Mary Magdalene Street on the market; there was no sense keeping it. Greta made some money on that because there were still so few livable places available.

Greta called him out on the deck one evening and asked him to sit with her the way they did when they first started hanging out at the beach house, before they bought it and demo'd and refurbed it. He thought it was a little odd because she usually didn't ask, she just went outside, knowing that he would follow sooner or later. But this was different. She had her tea and she was holding it with two hands, and she was not making eye contact. She was acting like a child and it made Vaughn nervous.

"Sure," he said. "Let me get a drink and I'll be out."

He took a long look in the liquor cabinet, then the refrigerator, finally picking a drink called Grapette out of the fridge. They'd bought a six-pack of this stuff because Greta remembered it from her childhood. "It's almost art by now," she had said.

"So, what's the deal?" he said, coming out the front door to the rebuilt deck. It was a pretty night, just going dark, heavy clouds in the west and behind them to the north, and lighter ones out east. On the news the guy had said that weather was blowing in from every direction.

"Nothing," she said. "I thought we'd sit a minute, take in the night."

"Okay," he said, pulling up a chair and squaring it away facing right at the water.

She didn't say anything for a few minutes, just leaned on the rail looking out toward the Gulf. After a while she turned her back to the water and faced Vaughn.

"I've been thinking," she said.

"There's trouble," he said. "I wish you wouldn't do that." She smiled and he shrugged, as if to apologize for the lame joke. "You're making me nervous," he said. "What's going on?"

She pushed off the railing and sat down next to him in her chair, taking a gulp of her tea. "I don't know," Greta said. "I've just been wanting to talk more with you. You know, figure things out. Get things settled or something."

"I thought things were settled," Vaughn said.

"Maybe they are," she said.

Vaughn was getting that hollow feeling in the pit of his stomach, and it was growing with every word she said. Something was wrong and he did not know what it was, had not seen it coming. It struck him suddenly that she wasn't as comfortable or satisfied with their new arrangement as he thought she was. Maybe all the stuff with Gail had taken its toll on her, shown her things that she hadn't wanted to see, betrayed him in some way. Maybe she was ready to move on, get back to work, recalibrate her life without him. The thought filled him with foreboding. He said, "I thought we'd talked about everything."

"Not everything," Greta said.

Now he was sure the way this was going, and he could not think of any way to disturb the path. He said, "I'm not going back. I mean, even if she comes back. I told you."

"I know," she said. "It's not about Gail."

He took a long swallow of the Grapette and the sweetness of the drink shocked him, flooded his brain with a syrupy grape sensation that made him wince. He looked at the bottle. "What's with this, anyway? It's crazy tasting."

"I know," Greta said. "That's why I wanted it. The bottles used to be real little. I can't believe you never had it."

"I had grape drinks, just not this one. This one's like eighty percent sugar or something. This is blood poison."

"It's good for you," she said, reaching for the bottle. She took a hit off it and swished it in her mouth, then swallowed. "A lost thing," she said.

"So, anyway, I don't know," Vaughn said. "I thought we were kind of settled in here. I thought this was working for both of us."

"Almost," Greta said. "There are some things hanging out there. I need to do some work, I mean, more work."

"That's good," he said. "You want to set up an office in town or something?"

She shook her head. "Not really. That's not the problem, anyway."

There it was. As clear a statement as she could have made. *That's not the problem, anyway.* Meaning there *was* a problem. He figured he'd go straight at it. No reason to try to dodge the bullet at this late date.

"What, then? You wish you hadn't sold the house? I suppose we should have waited. You know, set things up and tried 'em out before eliminating the support system."

"Not it," she said. "Worse."

"Okay," he said. He decided to wait for her.

"It's just that there're things you don't quite know, and before we get too comfortable I want to clear the air." She stood again and went back to the railing, looking out.

"You're not leaving?" he said.

She turned around, the wind pushing her T-shirt against her chest, bits of hair going around her head like tiny Japanese string kites. "I wasn't planning on it," she said.

"Well, what then?" he said.

"Okay. Here goes. You know all that stuff with me and Bo? In the paper? The cops, the arrest, all that?"

"Yes. I know all that."

She scratched her forehead with her fingertips, pushed her hair around a little, had an argument with the wind. Finally she said, "Well, they could have something."

He looked at her for a long time, seeing her against the sky, against the deck railing, the water, seeing her hair blow, and he didn't move. When he caught up with himself he was staring at her knees. He said, "Really." It was a question, and it wasn't.

She didn't move. She just watched him, her face poised, composed, artificial, like a replica of herself.

Vaughn shook his head slightly, an inch in either direction, then stopped that, looked back at her, carefully, at her eyes. She stood at the deck railing maybe seven feet away with the dark sky behind her, and all the sounds out there were suddenly distinct—the screech of seagulls, the light lap of the water on the sand, the white noise of the wind, the pipes jumping under the beach house as the dishwasher went through its cycle. *All that stuff with me and Bo.*

He finally looked away, rubbed his eyes, felt the wind

slipping by. He could feel blood pulsing in his neck. Greta was staring at him now, her gaze level, flat. A cold stare. She wasn't pleading, she wasn't even asking. She was just waiting, waiting for the message.

After another minute or two he pushed himself up out of the deck chair. "Well," he said finally. "You look good out here in the open. You're a good woman. I'd like you to stay with me, if you wouldn't mind."

He crossed the deck and put his arms around her waist and she put her arms around his shoulders and they stood like that for a few minutes, each looking at the other as if looking in a mirror. Then he looked away for a minute, and back at her, and then her eyes softened and lowered.

One afternoon in March Newton and Gail showed up in a Chrysler Crossfire, which was a two-seater not-quite-sports car they'd rented. Vaughn invited them in, offered them a drink, and then the four of them were sitting around in the living room when Gail told Vaughn and Greta that she and Newton were on their way to China to pick up a Chinese child they'd arranged to adopt.

"We have to get her and get it all done before May," Gail said. "They've got new rules on adoption over there. After May you're going to have to be a lot younger than we are."

"And prettier, too," Newton said.

Vaughn laughed politely and nodded, as if he knew what Gail was talking about. "So you're stopping off here on your way to China," he said.

"I just had to get some things, make some arrangements," Gail said. "You know."

"This is a great place," Newton said, waving at the room.

"Thanks," Greta said. "We did some of the work ourselves."

"She did," Vaughn said. "I supervised."

He was surprised by the idea of Gail and Newton adopting a Chinese child, but both of them looked so relaxed and excited that some of it rubbed off on him. He asked a few questions, had trouble following the answers because it seemed an enormously complicated process, and they'd apparently been at it awhile. Gail talked about what they were planning, how they'd set up Newton's house for the child, how old the child was, and where in China they were going to get her. She was sort of like the best Gail, kind of enthusiastic and involved and irrepressible, happy. Newton was friendly and calm in a way that seemed fresh, as if their time together, and their plans, suited him perfectly. And the mood was catching. What was so odd was that Vaughn felt none of the stress or threat or demand or sadness that had characterized the last act of their marriage. It was as if he was talking to genuine old friends, as if Newton, for years his envied and almost despised sibling, was now, suddenly, his dear younger brother again. Vaughn felt pleased for them, so much so that he was almost giddy.

When they were leaving, Vaughn hugged Gail, and it was the first time he'd hugged her with any feeling in a very long time. He took in her scent and enjoyed the warmth of her against him. He whispered, "I am so pleased for you."

She grinned and pulled away, whispering her thank-you.

Vaughn and Greta walked down to the car with them, everyone shook hands and hugged again, and then Gail and Newton jumped in the roadster and sped off up the coast highway, waving over their heads.

Vaughn went out to the end of the oyster shell driveway to fetch the empty garbage can, found the lid and put it on, and wheeled the big Rubbermaid can back up the drive to its spot on the concrete pad under the house.

Then the two of them went upstairs, got fresh drinks, and sat on the deck with Monkey and Fuzzy. After a bit Greta said, "I guess you're a *colossal* failure now."

"It's true," he said. "Newton has succeeded yet again. Hugely."

"I'm happy for Newton," Greta said. "And you are, too, aren't you? I could tell. You liked him."

"Well, I didn't *like* him, but, I mean—"

"Liked him," she said. "You liked them both. It was visible. Everybody knew it. It was unmistakably clear."

"Well, sure," Vaughn said. "How could you not? They're doing great. They're fine. And this baby thing is completely wacky."

"Not a baby," Greta said. "A young girl. Weren't you listening?"

"Kind of," he said.

"A lovely young girl," Greta said.

"Wacky," he said.

In the days that followed the weather was still and pleasant and most times both dogs seemed content to drop their heads on their paws and listen to the surf, as if they'd been doing that for a lifetime. Vaughn and Greta went about their lives in the reconstructed beach house, staying low, sticking to the shadows, as some wise coworker had once advised. Life was unmistakably quiet.

One night Vaughn had this dream: He came home to a tall Carpenter Gothic bungalow where he, apparently, lived. It was, of all places, on the seawall, the concrete buttress that jutted out against the anger of the ocean. It was a place he had never been. In that house he found his withered father with his brother, Newton, having one of their talks in the parlor. Vaughn stopped for a few minutes to chat with them, and his father, on hearing from Vaughn some report of his recent doings, made a demeaning crack at Vaughn's expense, about which the three of them shared a chuckle. The remark wasn't terribly serious, a routine aside, and when it passed Vaughn could not call it back to mind, could only sense the hollow place where the laughter had been, and the pleasure and the pain, as his brother and father enjoyed this harmless play. So Vaughn smiled then and moved through the room and into the kitchen where he set about preparing dinner for three, working a large pot on the stove with a heavy wooden spoon, standing and stirring a dramatic soup, listening to Newton and his father chattering away in the next room like the oldest and dearest friends. Vaughn stood over the ancient cream-colored stove edged in black, stirring and listening, not quite able to make out the words, but reassured by the tone, the familiarity, the confidence and comfort of the talk, the creaks of the old chairs in the house, and the sounds of the windows shifting against their sills. Then it was quiet and he heard his father's footsteps coming in from the parlor, and then his father was right alongside him at the stove, very close, so close that he could be smelled, so close Vaughn could sense his father's thick, rubbery skin, the age on him. And then his father, a short man with bright, rimless glasses, stood on tiptoes, his mouth inches away from Vaughn's ear, and said in the smallest of whispers, "Vaughn. I'm going to go now. See you soon."

About a month after Gail's visit they got a postcard with

a picture of Gail and Newton holding hands with a lovely Chinese child on the Great Wall. The three of them shining like all get-out, surrounded by mountaintops crested by the ribbon of the wall. They all looked so happy. Vaughn took the card into the kitchen and put it on the refrigerator with a magnet. The picture made him smile—*grin* was more like it. The child was sweet, a darling girl of maybe four or five. Newton looked more than ever like their father, looked generous yet intense. It was startling to see the resemblance, as if it had just emerged. Gail was simply radiant. The photograph filled Vaughn with pleasure. Greta came in and they stood together in the kitchen staring at the Chinese postcard of these charmed people and their new child atop the ancient wall. Vaughn turned the postcard over so Greta could read the message, scrawled in Gail's hand, on the front: *Some things are so perfect in this world. Some are so hard to arrange.* He imagined what his life with Greta might be in the future— isolated, inconsequential, apart from the world and yet in the world in a new, more immediate way, full of sensory things, a sampler of ordinary pleasures. He imagined their daily life as an endless succession of such pleasures, a river of tiny recognitions—the pleasures of toast, the pleasures of hot sunlight, of the dark scent of wet dogs, of summer nights, of the crush of sudden thunder, the warmth of winter socks, the surprise of skin indented by furniture. These weren't pleasures he had dreamed of, and it wasn't a life he had dreamed of, nor sought, nor even imagined for himself; but facing it, finally, he thought it was a life for which he was now well prepared.